A Terrifying Taste of
Short & Shivery

A TERRIFYING TASTE OF SHORT & SHIVERY

Thirty Creepy Tales

Retold by Robert D. San Souci

Illustrated by Lenny Wooden

Delacorte Press

Published by
Delacorte Press
Bantam Doubleday Dell Publishing Group, Inc.
1540 Broadway
New York, New York 10036

Library of Congress Cataloging-in-Publication Data
San Souci, Robert D.
      A terrifying taste of short & shivery : thirty creepy
tales / retold by Robert D. San Souci.
          p.   cm.
      Summary: A collection of scary traditional tales from
all over the world, including "Apparitions" from
Germany, "The Hundredth Skull" from Ohio, and "The
Ogre's Arm" from Japan.
      ISBN 0-385-32635-1
      1. Ghost stories.   2. Tales.   [1. Ghosts—Folklore.
2. Folklore.]   I. Title.
PZ8.1.S227An   1998
[398.25]—dc21   98-5551
                                                                CIP
                                                                 AC

The text of this book is set in 12-point New Baskerville.

Book design by Ericka L. Meltzer

Manufactured in the United States of America

October 1998

10   9   8   7   6   5   4   3   2   1

BVG

To Ray and Gail Orwig,
fellow fans of matters
science-fictional,
fantastical,
and
frightful

Contents

Introduction

Since you're reading these words, I think I can assume you have an appetite for terrifying tales. So I'll invite you to step up for a heaping helping of some of my scariest stories ever—spiced with shudders from near and far. There's something here for every taste; just hope nothing disagrees with you the way poor Aaron's curious meal does in "A Fish Story."

The poet Lord Byron once wrote, "Since Eve ate apples, much depends on dinner." And if you don't believe this, just ask an African *mulombe,* a Japanese ogre, an Australian Yara-ma-yha-who, or one of the other creatures in these pages. Of course, *their* favorite main course is the lonely wayfarer, the devil-may-care dare-taker, the overeager explorer, or the unlucky person who follows the wrong road or opens the wrong door. As someone pointed out, "You are what you eat (or what eats you)."

Put another way, "You're either the diner or the dinner." This fact is well illustrated in some of these stories. There's a monstrous pumpkin with a taste for people pie; a ghostly fox that turns the tables on two headstrong hunters and bags their spirits like so much soul food; and a were-tiger that gives a hair-raising twist to the notion of a family dinner. And there are some stories in which food tips the scales in favor of an intended victim: For example, a witch is undone by her undying love for the sweet, apple-like *zapotes* in a story from El Salvador.

Be warned: Nothing that's served up here is quite what it seems. A lavish wedding banquet, hosted by some rather ominous villagers, turns out to be more a feast for the eye than the taste buds. A simple meal of boiled halibut that a Tlingit Indian couple share with a ghost becomes the first course in a series of eerie encounters with the undead.

Not all these tales have to do with diners or dinners, but they're flavored with a teaspoon of thrills, a cup of chills, a soupçon of shivers, and a garnish of gallows humor. I hope you'll enjoy the smorgasbord of weird world tales I've prepared. In fact, I hope you'll find them frightfully tasty.

Bone appetit!

Crooker Waits

(British Isles—England)

Late in the afternoon a traveler on his way to the town of Cromford met an old woman in green skirts and a shawl.

"Where are you bound with the day so far gone?" she asked. "The sun will soon set, and this road is dangerous at night."

"My mother lies ill in the town ahead," he answered. "I must get there without delay."

"Have a care," the old woman said. "Crooker lies in wait. But it may be I can help." She reached into a pouch that hung from her belt and held out a sprig of St. John's Wort. The bright yellow flower seemed to glow in the late-afternoon sun.

Knowing it was a good-luck charm, the man took the old woman's offering, saying, "Thank you for your help."

"Your kindness has earned it," she explained. "You once freed a bird caught in a fowler's snare. I know that bird. As you travel the road, show the flower to Crooker."

"Who is Crooker?" the man asked.

But the old woman had vanished.

The man continued on his way. Near dusk, he rounded a bend in the lane and discovered another old woman, also dressed in green, waiting for him.

"The Cromford Road is dangerous at night," she told him. "Turn aside and go no farther before sunrise."

"My old mother is ill and needs me," he replied. "I cannot delay."

She nodded, then held out a handful of primroses to him, saying, "These are payment for freeing a rabbit from a snare. I know that rabbit. Show them to Crooker, who waits."

"Who is Crooker?" the man asked.

But she too was gone. The traveler shivered as shadows lengthened across the lonely road. Carefully he put the pale pink flowers in his pocket. Then he hurried on his way.

The sun had just set behind the hills when the man met a third old woman dressed in green. "It's a dark and dangerous time to be abroad on the Cromford Road," she said. "But it may be that these will help." She held out a bunch of bright yellow daisies to him. In the sun's afterglow, they seemed to burn like flames.

"You freed a fox and her cub from a trap," the old woman said. "I know that vixen and her cub. Take the flowers and show them to Crooker. But be sure you are on Cromford Bridge before the moon rises."

Then, like the others, she vanished even as he asked her, "Who is Crooker?"

The sun was completely gone now, and the moon had not yet risen. The traveler made his way slowly through the dark. Always, he was on the alert for Crooker, but he neither saw nor heard the fellow.

By the time he was in sight of Cromford Bridge, the moon had risen high and bright. He remembered the third woman's warning that he should be on the bridge before moonrise, but he felt himself out of danger. Nothing and no one lay between him and the bridge, save a great yew tree beside the road. In the moonlight, its crooked branches cast shadows that looked like swarms of skinny arms with clawed and clutching hands.

"You're letting imagination run off with you," the man said aloud. "Those old women were well-meaning, but their warnings have spooked you, sure enough."

He hastened forward. But as he passed through the shadow of the tree, a wind set the branches swaying and the leaves seething. The shadow claws fell all around him; and the wind through the leaves seemed to moan, *"Hungryhungryhungry."*

Suddenly a branch raked the man's cheek; a second slashed at him, drawing blood. To his horror, the tree seemed to twist and bend as though it were alive. The thick trunk leaned toward him. The branches—more like arms now—caught at his hair and cloak. *"Hungry-hungryhungry,"* the leaves murmured.

"Crooker!" gasped the man as he became ensnared. Desperately he reached into his pocket and pulled out the bunch of daisies. In his hand, the flowers flared into a cold yellow flame.

The tree branches snapped away; the leaves hissed and shrank back. Instantly the wind snuffed out the flame. But in that moment, the terrified man began running for the safety of the bridge.

He had only gone a little way when moonlight cast the shadow of reaching arms over him. Turning, he saw to his horror that the yew tree was now rooted in the road right behind him. While the leaves voiced their monstrous hunger, the man felt himself caught and lifted from the ground, drawn back toward the tree trunk.

Only with a great effort did he manage to draw the knot

of primroses from his pocket. These flared more brightly than the daisies had. Though the unearthly flame was cool to his fingers, it set the branches that held him ablaze and the leaves to shrieking. The burning limbs dropped him to the ground before the wind extinguished the fire.

Stunned, the man staggered on. But just before he flung himself onto the safety of the bridge, the clutching shadows fell over him again. With a sob, he realized that the great yew tree was now rooted at the foot of the bridge, like some terrible guardian.

Before the branches could catch him, the traveler hurled the sprig of St. John's Wort straight at the wicked tree. For a moment nothing happened. Then, deep inside the menacing tangle of branches, fire flared as bright as a thousand rising suns. It fountained up from root to treetop, turning each limb into a burning brand with flames for leaves. From the heart of the blaze came hundreds of screams turned into one deafening sound.

Pressing his hands to his ears, the traveler leapt onto the bridge. He fell badly, hitting his head against the stonework and knocking himself unconscious.

When he awoke, the sun had risen. Nearby, where the bridge met the riverbank, the charred stump of an ancient yew tree sent wisps of smoke into the chill morning air.

Yara-ma-yha-who

(Australia)

Long ago, there were two brothers, Perindi and Harrimiah, who always played and hunted together. This was a good thing, because the place where they lived was plagued by the Yara-ma-yha-who, little manlike creatures. They captured lone hunters, fed upon them, then turned them into Yara-ma-yha-who. They lived mostly in thick, leafy trees, but the wild fig tree was their favorite. When an adult or child took shelter from the summer sun in a fig tree's shade, or hid from winter's rain and hail under its thick boughs, the Yara-ma-yha-who would catch them.

Again and again, their grandmother warned the brothers to keep near each other, and to stay away from fig trees. Harrimiah always obeyed; but his older brother, Perindi, laughed at their grandmother's words. "The Yara-ma-yha-who do not exist," he said. "They are only stories told to make naughty children obey."

One day, when the brothers had been hunting far from their tribe's camp, Perindi said, "The sun is too hot to bear. There's a big fig tree beyond those rocks. Let's go sit in its shade, and eat some of its fruit. There's even a water hole near it."

But Harrimiah would not go: He was afraid that the lone tree might be home to some Yara-ma-yha-who. His brother mocked him, calling him a coward who was afraid of stories that only scared little children. Then the brothers argued for the first time in their lives. Angrily Harrimiah started for home, while Perindi, also in a temper, marched toward the distant fig tree.

But a drink of the water and the cool shade of the tree quickly put him in better spirits. Still thinking his brother a fool, Perindi lay down his spear, leaned back against the tree trunk, and chewed on a sweet fig.

Suddenly a lone Yara-ma-yha-who, who lived in the tree's branches, dropped from above onto Perindi's back and sent the boy sprawling in the dust. Shaking his head, Perindi saw in front of him a manlike creature about four feet high. It had red skin and glowing red eyes, and a very big head for its small body. Its jaws and stomach were quite large, but strangest of all were its hands: The fingertips were cup-shaped, like the suckers of an octopus. So were the tips of its toes.

Before Perindi could reach for his spear, the manikin pounced on him like a cat upon a mouse. When its fingers and toes touched the boy's shoulders and stomach, Perindi felt a series of little stings. Then he sensed his blood being drawn from his body through the suckers. He felt himself quickly growing weaker, until he was helpless to resist or even to move.

Just when Perindi thought he must die, the creature released him. Never taking its eyes off the boy, the Yara-ma-yha-who walked around and around him. Every time it passed in front of Perindi, the boy saw the creature's eyes were filled with fresh hunger.

At last it stopped and lay down on the ground facing Perindi. To the boy's horror, he saw the great jaws, hinged like a snake's, spread wide, wider—

Slup! The Yara-ma-yha-who swallowed Perindi to his knees. Then the creature stood up, and danced up and down until it had settled the boy all the way into its stomach. Then it went to the water hole, where it drank and drank. Finally it lay down on the ground again, and spit the boy out.

Perindi was still alive, though weak as a newborn pup. And he was smaller. He tried to crawl away, but the Yara-ma-yha-who swallowed him—*slip-slup!*—down again. This time the boy, grown smaller, was an easier meal.

Again the creature drank water until it was nearly bursting, and again it lay down and spit out the dazed Perindi. The boy was smaller yet, but still alive.

Now while this was happening, Harrimiah, sensing that his brother might be in trouble, had returned in time to see the manikin swallow Perindi—*slip!*—a third time. Raising his spear, he charged the creature. But the Yara-ma-yha-who scurried into the safety of the leafy tree.

Harrimiah shouted and jabbed the green shadows, but all he heard was the rustle of leaves as the creature avoided his spearpoint.

Finally, tired from his efforts and grieving for his lost brother, Harrimiah turned to collect dry brush, planning to burn down the tree and destroy the beastling.

At that moment, the Yara-ma-yha-who dropped onto his back. The impact threw the boy to the ground, where he hit his head on a stone and was knocked unconscious.

When he came to, Harrimiah watched the Yara-ma-yha-who return from the water hole, lie down, and spit out Perindi a third time. Now the boy seemed hardly bigger than an infant. And he was as bald and smooth-skinned as a baby. His skin was pale, as though all the color had been drained from it. With a grunt and a nod, the Yara-ma-yha-who turned away from what was left of Perindi. Keeping his eyes nearly closed, Harrimiah was able to see the creature walking toward him.

But he remembered his grandmother's warning: "If you cannot escape the Yara-ma-yha-who, you must pretend to be dead. The creature only hunts the living. You must keep still, no matter what the Yara-ma-yha-who does to make sure you are dead. It will poke you and tickle you. If you don't move, it will go away and hide and spy on you. If you keep still until it is dark, the thing will go to sleep. Then you can escape."

True enough, the Yara-ma-yha-who picked up a stick and poked Harrimiah in the side. The boy did not flinch. Then the creature tickled him under the neck and arm. The boy remained motionless, his eyes tightly closed. One last time the creature poked the boy, then tickled him. When its victim neither moved nor made a sound, it went behind the trunk of the fig tree to watch.

Through the hot afternoon, even when insects crawled across his skin, Harrimiah remained like one dead. When night fell, the boy quietly climbed to his feet. He took his spear and circled the fig tree.

The Yara-ma-yha-who was asleep against the trunk. Harrimiah finished the creature with a single thrust of his spear. Then he went and knelt beside his brother.

Perindi was still alive. His eyes were open. When he opened his mouth to speak, he made soft mewling sounds like a baby. His skin was darker now, with a reddish tint.

Harrimiah scooped up the tiny Perindi. Clutching his brother to his chest, the boy fled across the moon-streaked desert. But as he ran, he felt the form in his arms changing. Perindi's head was growing bigger, while his legs and arms seemed to be growing smaller.

Suddenly Harrimiah cried out as something stung his chest like bees. Looking down, he saw that his brother had pressed his small fingers against Harrimiah's skin. The ends of those fingers had turned to suckers, as had his toes.

Harrimiah pulled the hands away from his skin with little *poppl*ing sounds. Then he tossed the thing onto the sand and began running for his life. He easily escaped, for the Yara-ma-yha-who cannot run very fast on their tiny legs. Harrimiah looked back only once, to see the creature his brother had become glaring furiously after him, red eyes blazing with hunger.

The Fata

(Italy)

One evening, three girls from a small town near Torino sat spinning. The moon was full, casting a curious bright light over everything. This started the two youngest, Maria and Stella, talking about ghosts and various strange creatures. As the spinning wheels whirred, they spoke of *folletti,* the little sprites that have magic powers and can cause nightmares or madness if angered.

"Stop talking such nonsense!" ordered the oldest girl, Barbarina. "There are no such things as *folletti!*"

"You shouldn't talk that way," warned Maria. "The *folletti* may hear and punish you."

"I don't believe in such things," insisted Barbarina. "They're just tales for grandmothers to tell by the fireside."

"Well, *I* believe in them. The same as I believe in the *fata,*" said Stella. "She can live in the wood or the river or the sea. My brother is a sailor. He has seen the palace of Fata Alcina shimmering in the air above the Strait of Messina."

"He saw a mirage. Or he imagined it," said Barbarina with a sniff. "If it was real, why didn't he pay a visit to the *fata?*"

"Oh, no!" cried Stella, "Any sailor who tries to reach her castle will be lost at sea."

"I think I would like to meet a *fata,*" said Maria. "My grandmother—"

Here Barbarina just sighed and shook her head.

Maria ignored her and continued, "Granny knew a man who stopped to help an old woman carry a sack of kindling in the forest. Suddenly the old woman turned into a tall, beautiful lady dressed in white. The *fata* thanked him for his kindness, then vanished. When he looked in the sack, he found that the kindling had turned to gold coins."

"Fairy tales!" exclaimed Barbarina.

"If I met a *fata,*" said Stella, "I would want her to give me great beauty."

"You should ask for brains," said Barbarina. "You both could use them more than gold or beauty, if you believe such nonsense."

For a time, an angry silence settled over the room. There was just the sound of the three spinning wheels humming away.

At last, ignoring Barbarina, Maria said to Stella, "Certain people don't want to hear things. But my granny says a *fata* lives in the big chestnut tree on the hill at the center of the forest."

Stella looked out the window at the moon-drenched countryside. "I'm certain that if anyone were brave enough to go into the woods when the moon is as bright as it is tonight, that person would see the *fata.*"

"Just to show you how foolish you are," said Barbarina, "I'll go out there alone tonight and prove she doesn't exist!"

Her friends were shocked.

"Don't anger the *fata*," Maria cautioned.

"If you displease her," added Stella, "she'll give you bad luck or worse."

Barbarina picked up her sharp-pointed spindle. "I will leave this as proof that I have been there. You can see for yourself tomorrow, when daylight gives you courage." Then out the door she went. Her friends called to her and begged her to come back, but she didn't even turn around.

The other girls waited anxiously for her to return.

The morning came, but Barbarina did not.

Summoning some neighbors, Maria and Stella organized a search party.

They soon found the missing girl. Barbarina lay under the giant chestnut tree, with her spindle thrust through her heart.

The Fiddler

(British Isles—Wales)

Deep in the steep, rugged Welsh hills lies a certain cave. Its mouth is largely hidden by thick, rank grass and briars that grow undisturbed, tangling and strangling each other. For as long as anyone can remember, folks have said it is dangerous to approach within five paces of the opening.

Once, a fox with a pack of hounds in close pursuit ran straight for the entrance. Suddenly the fox turned right around, with its fur all bristling in terror, and ran back into the middle of the pack. The hunters later said it had struck them that, to the fox, anything earthly—even an earthly death—seemed preferable to the unearthly horrors of the cave. But the fox escaped, for not a dog would go near it. It was aglow with green, yellow, and blue lights, as though a swarm of will-o'-the-wisps were clinging to its fur.

Many years ago, there was a shepherd, Elias Ifan, who had a friend named Ned Pugh. Ned was a fiddler who earned his keep by playing at weddings and dances and other gatherings.

One evening Elias was sitting in the local tavern when Ned came in. He was in unusually high spirits, and paid for a round of drinks.

"Come into a bit of good fortune, have you?" asked Elias.

"That I have," Ned agreed.

"And can you tell me the source of it?" asked Elias.

"That I cannot," Ned told his friend. Shortly after this, he paid the barkeeper and went on his way. Elias saw a puzzled look on the barkeeper's face. When he asked what was the matter, the man just showed him the coin the fiddler had paid him with. To Elias's surprise, the coin proved to be solid gold, and ancient.

The next day, and the day after that, Ned spent more of the gold coins. But he refused to tell Elias where they had come from, and Elias grew more and more curious.

On All Hallows' Eve, Elias was returning home in the misty twilight. His dog trotted beside him. By chance, he passed about a hundred yards from the haunted cave. Faintly he heard a fiddle playing a strange tune. Rounding a large boulder, Elias was startled to see Ned facing the cave's mouth, his fiddle at his chest. As he played, he danced a jig, his legs moving tirelessly.

To his horror, Elias realized that Ned was within the fatal five paces of the cave. He shouted and shouted to the man until the rocks echoed around him, but Ned Pugh seemed perfectly deaf: He fiddled and danced away without a care.

Though he dreaded the cave, Elias could not leave his friend in such danger. He edged as near as he could, hoping to pull the fiddler away with his long shepherd's crook.

But when he was almost near enough to reach his friend, Elias stopped and stared. Beyond the dancing man, the cave was ablaze with swirling and darting will-o'-the-wisps, glowing green, yellow, and blue. Amid the fairy lights, a company of tall men and women, clothed in ele-

gant robes, danced to Ned's music. They were watched over by a shadowy figure seated on a gold throne at the back of the cave. Though he couldn't see the seated person clearly, Elias was suddenly transfixed with terror. He felt he could count every upright hair on the back of his dog, which crouched and quivered between his legs.

All the while, Ned fiddled and danced with his back to the shepherd.

With a great effort, Elias forced his fear-stricken muscles to move, and he stretched out his crook to his friend. Hooking the sleeve of Ned's jacket, Elias began to pull him to safety. Even as he was tugged away from the cave, Ned kept on playing and dancing his mad little jig.

Suddenly there was a howl from the cave. A blast of cold wind tore Elias's cap from his head. His dog fled, but Elias found himself rooted to the spot.

Still Ned fiddled and capered. Behind him, the tall dancers had changed into hideous cavorting demons and imps. The shadowy figure on the throne was growing larger, revealing a misshapen body, and a swollen head from which two baleful red eyes burned into Elias's own.

Desperately Elias gave a final tug on his crook. The motion swung the fiddler around, though it did not quite pull him out of the fatal zone.

With a groan, Elias saw that Ned's face was as pale as marble, his eyes were staring as fixedly as one dead, and his head was dangling loose on his shoulders. He was still fiddling, but his arms kept the fiddlestick in motion without consciousness on Ned's part. In the same way his legs were moving like a puppet's, jerked by invisible strings.

The howling from the cave grew so loud that Elias, still frozen to the spot, dropped the crook and clapped his hands over his ears. At that moment, the dark figure inside the cave waved a hand grown huge and clawed.

The will-o'-the-wisps were extinguished. The cave became as black as the very mouth of Hades, save for two fiery eyes.

As the terrified shepherd watched, the fiddler's body became thin and transparent. Still fiddling and capering, Ned Pugh was sucked into the cave in the same way that summer mist is drawn up by the rising sun.

In an instant he was gone, and with him, his music. The red eyes blinked out. Elias felt his legs buckle under him, dropping him to his knees. After a moment, he found he could stand up. Then he took off for home, never once looking back.

Ned Pugh was never seen again. But folks say that on All Hallows' Eve a person with enough courage to approach the entrance of the cave will hear Ned playing. And on certain nights in leap year, they add, a watcher can even see him. Amid blazing will-o'-the-wisps and shadowy dancers, the wretched fiddler scrapes and capers—and may well go on dancing and fiddling for all eternity.

Land-Otter

(Native American—Tlingit tribe)

The Tlingit live on the northwest coast of America, relying on the sea to provide much of their food. One year, however, the halibut grew scarce. The people took their boats out every day, but their lines and nets turned up few fish.

A certain man and his wife built a little house for themselves far from the village of Silka, just out of reach of the high tides. They fished tirelessly, but the halibut seemed to be growing scarcer; the one or two small fish they caught in a week hardly kept them alive. The wife would go to the beach at low tide and look for crabs or shrimp in the pools among the rocks; but even so, the couple grew thinner and thinner.

One night the husband came home with only one little halibut in his big fishing basket. They were both very hungry and could have eaten ten fish each. Even so, the woman only put part of the halibut in the pot that stood on the fire; she hung the rest of it outside in a shed. "At least there will be something for us to eat tomorrow," she said.

But when the morning came, the couple heard a strange noise in the shed, as if someone were throwing things around.

"What is that?" asked the wife. "Let's go and see who

has got into the shed." But they found no one. Instead they discovered, to their surprise, the large, flat shapes of two devilfish on the floor.

"How did they come up from the beach?" the woman asked. "Someone must have carried them."

"It doesn't matter," her husband said. "Whoever brought them was very kind. Now we have good bait to help us catch some halibut."

But the woman, in a voice little more than a whisper, said, "I know who brought them here. Last night I had a dream about our son, who drowned last year. He said he knows how poor we are, and that he has taken pity on us. He told me that if I hear anyone whistle, I must call his name, Land-Otter."

Then they put out to sea and baited their lines with pieces of the devilfish, and this time they caught two good-sized halibut. As soon as it grew dark, they rowed back and beached their canoe. The woman went inside and threw one of the halibut into the pot. At that moment, she heard a whistle behind the house, and her heart beat wildly.

"Come in, Land-Otter, my son," she cried. "We have missed you these many months. Do not be afraid; there is no one here except your father and me."

The whistle was repeated, but nobody entered. Then the man flung open the door and shouted, "Come in, my son! We are grateful for your help." And though neither the man nor his wife saw Land-Otter enter the house, they turned and discovered him sitting opposite them, by the fire, with his hands over his face.

"Is this truly you?" they asked. Again he whistled in answer. Then the three sat in silence until midnight, when the young man made some sounds through his hands, as if he would speak. Shifting himself so that his parents could not see his face, he pointed to the door. Opening it, the husband discovered two more devilfish. When he turned back, his son had covered his face.

"In the morning we will go out," Land-Otter said in a strange voice, as if speaking was difficult. Then he ran into the night. They saw his shadowy form racing toward the forest.

It was still dark when Land-Otter returned to the house and shook his father awake. "Get up, it is time to fish," he said. So they fetched the line and dragged the canoe to the water's edge. In the darkness, Land-Otter was only a dark shape. He seated himself at the front of the canoe. When his father was seated behind him, Land-Otter took a paddle and pulled so hard that they reached the feeding grounds of the halibut in a few minutes. After that, he baited the hooks and fastened the end of the line to the seat.

"Put the blanket over you," he told his father, always keeping his face turned away. "Do not watch me." But his father did watch him through a hole in the blanket. He saw his son get up very gently, so that the boat would not rock, and plunge into the sea. Secretly watching, he saw his son move swiftly through the water, catching halibut and placing them on the hooks. Then Land-Otter reboarded the canoe as carefully as he had left. But he kept his face turned away, though his father still had the blanket over him.

Land-Otter's father pretended to be asleep. When his son shook him, he yawned and stretched like one newly awakened. Then, always keeping his face averted, Land-Otter helped his father pull in one big halibut after another. The canoe was soon full, and they paddled home.

But the moment they touched the shore, Land-Otter

looked at the sky. "I must hurry to find shelter before the raven cries!" he exclaimed. Then he ran off to the woods, his hands shielding his face, while his father watched in surprise.

It took the couple all day to clean and salt the halibut so that they would always have something to eat. Darkness came before they finished. In the evening, they found their son in front of the fire, sitting with his back to them. The mother prepared a bowl of cooked fish and set it beside him, being careful not to look at his face. Land-Otter ate this eagerly.

So things continued for a week. Again and again, Land-Otter's parents begged him not to go back to the woods to sleep. After a time, he stayed with them. But he always slept beside the fire with his back to them.

Every day, before it was light, he would wake his father. Then they would go out fishing and always return with their canoe full of fish. Soon they had great stores of food.

Sometimes the mother would go with them, because she loved fishing. But both husband and wife were careful never to look at their son's face. Now Land-Otter let them watch him slip into the sea and harvest the halibut. But they turned away when he climbed back into the canoe.

Very soon, no longer fearing starvation, they packed up their store of food, put it in the canoe, and set off for Silka to return to their tribe. Land-Otter, wrapped in a blanket, sat at the front, with his parents behind him.

But as they drew near the landing place at Silka, the woman whispered to her husband, "What is the matter with our son? I can only see the shadow of his hands on the paddles."

Still the shadow-hands rowed steadily on. Land-Otter remained hunched under his blanket. Suddenly the blanket began to crumple as though Land-Otter had fainted. His anxious father grabbed the blanket and pulled it away.

At first they saw only a vague figure of mingled mist and shadow. The woman cried out, and the ghostly shape turned toward her. For a horrible moment the couple saw the drowned face of their son. His eyes were gone, his flesh had been picked nearly to the bone by fish, his long hair was tangled with the muck of the seabed.

Then he vanished. From the woods behind the village came the lonely cry of a raven, like a distant farewell.

A Fish Story

(United States—Virginia—African American traditional)

Long ago, down Virginia way, there was a young man, Aaron, who spent most of his Sundays with his fishing pole on the riverbank. He ignored the warnings of his family and friends and preacher, who told him it was bad luck to fish on the Sabbath.

"Fish ain't gonna bite," they warned him.

But Aaron caught strings of fish.

Then everyone told him, "Them fish gonna kill you if you eat 'em."

But Aaron ate the fish and felt as strong and healthy as ever. Maybe stronger.

After that, a lot of young folks got the idea that fishing—or doing other things—on the Sabbath might not be unlucky after all. But the old people still said, "Bad luck gonna come that boy's way sooner or later." When the preacher scolded him for his wicked ways, Aaron only laughed and said, "Mebbe it's time you got youse'f some new ideas. Don't seem nothin' bad gonna happen to me."

"Just you wait," the preacher warned.

Then, one Sunday when Aaron was out fishing, he sat for hours and hours without a single bite. He was just about to give up when he felt a slight tug on his line. His cork was yanked under the water, so he knew he had a bite.

Eagerly he pulled with all his might, but he found it difficult to haul the fish to the surface. He tugged and strained, and finally he flipped his catch out of the water and onto the bank beside him.

To his amazement, he found he had caught an animal unlike any he had ever seen. It had a head like a snapping turtle, wings like a duck, and a tail like a fish. Strangest of all, it had a human voice, and it sang him a greeting:

> *How do, Aaron?*
> *How do, Aaron?*

Frightened, the young man dropped his fishing pole and started up the bank as fast as his legs could carry him. But the animal sang after him:

> *Come back, Aaron,*
> *Come back, Aaron.*

Aaron found himself unable to resist, so back he came. Then the creature sang:

> *Pick me up, Aaron,*
> *Pick me up, Aaron.*

Aaron picked the animal up. Then it sang:

> *Carry me home, Aaron,*
> *Carry me home, Aaron.*

Aaron did as the thing ordered. When they got to Aaron's cabin, the animal sang:

Clean and cook me, Aaron,
Clean and cook me, Aaron.

Aaron cleaned it and put it on to cook, thinking that after the creature was in the pot, it would stop singing commands to him. But as soon as the turtle-duck-fish was cooked, it piped up from the pot:

Take me off, Aaron,
Take me off, Aaron.

Unable to disobey, Aaron took the thing off the stove, and set it on a big old plate. By now the young man was sweating with fear. He dreaded what he was afraid was coming. And—sure enough!—the steaming plateful sang:

Eat me up, Aaron,
Eat me up, Aaron.

Helpless, Aaron began to eat as he was commanded. But the awfulness of what he was doing stopped him after a mouthful or two. Still his dinner sang even more compellingly:

Eat me all up, *Aaron,*
Eat me all up, *Aaron.*

Forkful by forkful, Aaron ate every bite. As soon as he had finished the last mouthful, his stomach began to pain him something terrible. Then it began to swell up like a balloon.

Clutching his gut, Aaron ran into the yard, yelling, "I ate me something bad. It done poisoned me!"

His neighbors came running, along with the preacher, who cried, "Wickedness gonna catch up with a sinner sooner or later."

Meanwhile Aaron was rolling around in the dust. His stomach had swollen as big as if he'd swallowed the granddaddy of all pumpkins. Still it continued to grow—until he burst open.

Out came the turtle-duck-fish, whole and alive, looking the same as when Aaron had caught it. Hopping and flopping, it went back to the river, all the while singing:

> *Catch fish on Sunday, Aaron,*
> *And see what catches you!*

Aaron was laid to rest in the little cemetery by the riverbank. The preacher preached the story over and over again, reminding his flock to keep holy the Lord's Day. And that strange creature was never seen again in those parts.

Apparitions

(Germany)

In 1816, the king of Prussia paid a hurried visit to his favorite officer, Marshal Blucher, who had retired years before. The old soldier had sent word to the monarch that he was unwell and urgently wished to see his dear friend. Blucher's message pleaded with the monarch to visit him no later than August twelfth.

Court matters delayed the monarch's departure. He reached Blucher's castle at the stroke of midnight on the twelfth. Servants quickly led him to the library, where the old soldier, dressed in a heavy robe, sat in an armchair. A second chair was set beside the marshal's for the king. The ruler was startled to see that the man, once so rough and ready, had grown frail and infirm.

"What was so important that you had to see me right away?" the king asked kindly.

Blucher clutched his robe more tightly around his thin chest, then said, "I am not mad, but I have a terrible secret to reveal." As the hour grew later, he told his strange story.

When Blucher had been a lad of about sixteen, the Seven Years' War was raging across Europe, spreading ruin and death. The young man, born of a noble family, left his father's estate to join the Prussian cavalry. Events kept him away for more than a year. During this time, he had no word from his family. He grew increasingly worried when he learned that fierce fighting had taken place near his home.

At last he obtained several months' leave from his regiment. After a long journey, he arrived in the forest near his father's house during a raging storm. Just before midnight he reached home drenched to the bone. Jumping off his horse, he tried the door. It was locked. Losing patience, he hammered at the heavy oaken door with the end of his whip.

Suddenly the door swung open. To his surprise, young Blucher saw no one. Shouting, he hurried inside; but the halls and rooms were dark and silent. With a sinking heart, he guessed that the war had driven his family away. He decided to spend the night; the next day he would try to learn more about what had become of his parents and sisters.

But when he had climbed the stairs to the upper hall, he saw light under the closed door of his father's bedroom. Eagerly he entered. Inside, a faint and fitful flame in the fireplace threw a dim light over six seated figures. As one, his father, mother, and four sisters rose.

Blucher went to embrace his father, but the older man waved him away. Blucher held out his arms to his mother, but she backed off with a sad look. His sisters just stared at him a moment, then took each other by the hand and sat down again.

"Father, don't you know me?" the confused young man asked. "Mother, you are silent. Dear sisters, have you forgotten the laughter and childhood games we shared?"

At these last words, his sisters began whispering to

one another. Then each of them stood up and beckoned him closer. The youngest, Katrina, knelt down in front of their mother and hid her face at the woman's knee.

Blucher realized that the girl wanted to play a game they had played as children. With her eyes hidden, Katrina held her hand out, palm up. She would try to guess who touched it. The others stood watching, no one making a move to play. On impulse, Blucher lightly touched his sister's hand. Instantly she lifted her head and looked at him, nodding. Then she stood aside and indicated silently that he should take a turn.

The young man knelt before his mother. As he had often done as a child, he hid his face on her knee while he put out his hand.

To his horror, Blucher felt through her silk dress the cold hardness of bone. The room was now filled with a rattling sound. He was further startled when he felt a hand placed in his.

Looking up, he saw that he held a skeletal hand that had a gold bracelet circling the bit of wristbone. With a cry, he dropped it on the carpet in front of the now stone-cold fireplace. All trace of his family had disappeared, except for the delicate, gleaming bones in front of the empty chairs.

In a panic Blucher ran from the room, hurried out to his horse, and fled wildly through the forest. A low-hanging branch struck him unconscious from his mount. He was found by a hunter the next day and nursed back to health by the man's family. The horror of what he had seen troubled him more than his injuries.

Blucher learned that his family had perished in the war,

when enemy soldiers had raided the house. As soon as he was strong enough, he returned to search for the bodies of his family, to give them a proper burial. But all he found was the single skeletal hand, encircled by its gold bracelet, which lay where he had dropped it. This he took and sealed in the wall of the family chapel.

"Many years have glided by since that awful scene in my father's castle," Marshal Blucher said to the king of Prussia. "But now comes the reason I sent for you in such haste.

"Several days ago, while I was dozing in this armchair, a slight noise awoke me. I looked up and saw my father, mother, and sisters—just as they appeared on that terrible night. They joined hands and slowly circled my chair. This time they spoke, saying over and over, 'We'll meet again on the twelfth of August, at midnight!' Three times they moved around me, then faded into the air."

The old soldier shuddered and turned away. "I knew they were warning me of my approaching death. And I did not want to depart this world until I bade farewell to Your Majesty, my oldest and dearest friend."

But the king shook his head and said, "My dear marshal! What you've told me is very strange; but I believe the second visit was only a fever dream, caused by your illness. I am sure you will live many years yet."

The clock on the mantel struck three A.M. "You see!" the ruler exclaimed, "August twelfth is long past, and here we sit together. Now will you believe you imagined the ghostly warning?"

The king grasped the old man's hand to reassure him. The bones beneath the paper-thin skin were as chilled and stiff as rods of ice. "Your hands are as cold as the grave!" cried the king. But there was no answer. The king watched in horror as the skin began to crumble beneath his fingers, leaving him to hold the pale bones of a skeletal hand.

The Bijli

(India)

In 1890, Herbert Young, a Britisher living in India, set out on a hunt. He traveled on horseback, accompanied by several servants. At the end of the second day, worn out from long hours in the saddle, he decided to pitch camp near a little village. There was a large pool on the outskirts, shaded by a wide, leafy banyan tree.

While his servants prepared the evening meal, Young strolled along the edge of the pool. He discovered a *fakir*, a wandering holy man, sitting and staring at the water. The man wore only a loincloth, and his hair was long and matted, but he greeted Young politely. Then he said, "I beg you not to touch or drink this water, Sahib. If you do, evil will surely befall you."

When Young asked the reason for this warning, the man replied, "Many years ago a wicked man drowned in this pool. Anyone who drinks or bathes in this water will suffer for it."

Young thanked him, but gave no serious thought to what he believed was superstitious chatter. One of his servants overheard, however, and alerted the others. Though the Britisher drank the nearby pool's water and washed in it, his frightened servants brought water for their own use from a distant stream.

After a brief rest, Young decided to break camp and

travel on in the cool of the night. About three A.M., he and his bearers had reached the middle of a wide expanse of cotton fields. Far ahead, Young saw a tiny glimmer of light. At first he thought it was the light in some native hut. Then he noticed that it appeared to be moving rapidly toward them. It seemed to be a flaming torch, though he could not see who was carrying it.

To his astonishment, his bearers suddenly threw down the baggage they were carrying, crying, *"Bijli! Bijli!"*

Young knew the word meant "evil spirit." All around him, his men were running for their lives, away from the torch.

Cursing them for being such cowards, Young spurred his horse forward, toward the light. He could now see that the torch was being held by what looked like a man.

"Halt!" he cried in Hindi, as loudly as he could.

The person paid no attention to the shout. He came gliding along at the same speed. Suddenly Young's horse snorted, reared, and nearly unseated its rider. Trembling in every limb, the horse refused to move forward.

Determined to find out who the stranger was, Young dismounted to march on and meet the man on foot. The moment he released the reins, the frightened horse bolted, following the fleeing bearers.

Young sensed a threat in the onrushing flame, which was only a few yards away. He raised his rifle to his shoulder, crying, "Stand still, or I will fire at you!"

The words were hardly out of his mouth when he was horrified to see that the figure, which was flying along above the ground, was not a human being at all. All that was visible was a grinning, bony skull with empty eye sockets, long, streaming hair, and a fleshless arm holding a

flaming torch. The rest of the figure was a trail of gray mist.

Holding his ground, Young fired. His bullet didn't seem to strike the thing, but the apparition suddenly swerved a bit, then hurtled past the terrified man. About twenty feet behind him, the *bijli* suddenly dived earthward and vanished into the ground.

Shaking, Young went to the spot and stamped on the earth. It seemed solid. Only a sprinkling of red-hot embers marked the passage of the torch-bearing horror.

Young started back the way he had come, and soon found his horse grazing peacefully. Then, after much shouting, he located his bearers. They continued on their way, avoiding the haunted cotton fields.

Later, when they returned to the village by the fatal pool, a man told Young, "You were lucky, Sahib. Last year a traveler who drank from the pool was found dead in the cotton fields you crossed. His face was horribly burned."

Before his meeting with the fiery figure, Young would have laughed at such talk. Now he felt a chill down his spine. He felt certain that if he had shown any trace of fear when face-to-face with the *bijli* of the flaming torch, or if it had even touched him, he would be a dead man.

The Lutin

(Canada—French Canadian traditional)

When the French came to Canada, they brought many traditions with them, including a belief in *lutins*. These goblins could take many forms, from giant spiders to small humans. They might help farmers by bringing good weather or by keeping the milk from souring, or they could cause great mischief. . . .

There was once an *habitant*, a farmer, named Louis, who had a splendid mare he called Ma Princesse, who was his pride. Each morning he would go to the stable to bring her fresh oats and water, tend her, then take her for a ride.

But one morning, he discovered Ma Princesse trembling with weariness, her flanks soaked with sweat, her muzzle flecked with foam. Clearly she had been ridden furiously during the night. Curiously, the mysterious rider had braided the horse's mane into tangled loops.

Louis soothed and groomed her, but he could not comb the loops out of her mane. That night he padlocked the stable securely. In the morning, he found the lock still securely fastened, though Ma Princesse was in the same exhausted state as the night before. This time one of her shoes was missing.

While the blacksmith in the nearby village was reshoeing his horse, Louis explained what had happened. Antoine, the blacksmith, nodded and said, "This is the work of a *lutin*. You must brand Ma Princesse with a cross. That will keep her safe. Then the loops will comb out when it rains again."

But Louis thought such stories were foolishness. "I am sure someone who is a clever picklock is coming by night to ride my mare. Perhaps he is jealous of Ma Princesse."

When he returned the mare to her stall, he tried and tried to untangle her mane. But the untidy loops came back no matter how hard he combed them out.

Still Louis refused to believe that a *lutin* was causing his troubles. He made up his mind to catch what he was sure would prove to be a human mischief-maker. So that night he kept watch from his bedroom window on the second floor of his house. From this vantage point, by the light of the full moon, he could clearly see the barn doors with the padlock in place.

Suddenly he heard the frightened neighing of Ma Princesse. To his astonishment, the padlock snapped open and the barn doors flew wide. Out galloped Ma Princesse, with something on her back that seemed as dark as the horse's coat.

The frantic horse raced toward the house on a course that would take her beneath the window where her owner stood. Louis was trembling now, because as the horse came nearer, he could see that the creature riding her was a small, horrible goblin covered with long, dark hair. Its apelike head had sharp white fangs, fiery yellow eyes, and horns like a goat. One clawed hand was tangled in Ma Princesse's mane, while the other lashed the horse's flank with a slender branch.

In a moment, the horse and the hideous rider would

pass beneath the window. Quickly Louis grabbed the little holy-water font that every devout *habitant* kept in his bedroom. He flung this at the goblin's head.

The font struck the creature on the forehead. It shrieked as the little stone bowl shattered, showering both the *lutin* and the horse with droplets of holy water. Where these touched the monster, its fur began to burn, and the skin beneath to sizzle. The thing howled and leapt about, driving Ma Princesse to a frenzy. Then the *lutin* burst into flame and vanished with a final, horrible scream.

For a moment Louis feared he had been blinded by the flash of devil's fire; then his sight returned. There was no trace of the creature. But the riderless, still terrified horse charged on into the night.

It was not till late the next day that Louis, with the help of his neighbors, found the horse in a distant meadow. Her dark coat was streaked with white sweat; her mane was still tangled in loops.

Louis was careful to brand her with a cross. And he had the village *curé*, its priest, bless the barn and sprinkle the horse with holy water.

No *lutin* ever came back to trouble Ma Princesse. And the next time it rained, Louis was able to comb the tangles out of the mare's mane. The farmer never doubted the old stories after that.

The Hundredth Skull

(United States—Ohio)

In the early 1800s, Bill Quick, a trapper and frontiersman, lived in a cabin on the upper Scioto River, near what is now the town of Kenton, Ohio. It was a time of hatred between many whites and Indians—hatred that often flared into violence.

One evening when Bill returned from hunting, he found his home ransacked and robbed of everything of value. Amid the wreckage his aged father lay dead, with an arrow in his heart. To Bill's horror, he saw that his parent had been scalped. The raging, grieving hunter vowed on the spot that he would avenge his father's death a hundred times over.

From that moment on, he became the deadly enemy of all Indians in the area—the guilty and the innocent. He secretly haunted the woodland paths and stream banks, killing any Indian man he chanced upon. Then he took the heads of his victims and put them on shelves he built in his cabin.

In time, he collected ninety-nine of these ghastly trophies. Row upon row of grinning skulls filled his shelves.

"Only one more skull to go," he muttered to himself. "Then my vengeance is complete."

But the Indians—aware of their danger—were keeping better guard. Many had already left the area.

Before the hundredth man fell to his rifle, Bill was seized with a fatal illness. He called his son, Tom, to his bedside. Pointing to the skulls, the dying man said, "You must fulfill the oath I took, by adding a hundredth skull to the others. If you fail, your murdered grandfather and I will come back to punish you."

"I promise," said Tom uneasily.

Shortly after this, Bill Quick died.

Tom tried to make good on his gruesome vow, but things always seemed to work against him. He wasn't much of a hunter, or a very good shot. He had no liking for violence. And the Indians had by now abandoned the region completely.

He kept putting off the unpleasant duty of filling the final space on the topmost shelf. When he felt guilty about failing to keep his promise to his father, he soothed his guilt with drink and gambling. As time went on, he caroused more and more and thought less and less about his promise.

One morning, Tom had returned home after a wild night of carrying on. The bleary-eyed man was nearly frightened out of his wits when the eye sockets of the skulls upon the shelves suddenly began to glow. Then they began to gibber and clack their teeth together. Certain the skulls were mocking his weakness, he cursed them, then fled into the daylight.

When Tom babbled out his story to his friends, they first decided he had gone mad. But when they learned his dark secret—that he was under oath to kill an Indian—they grew disgusted and shunned him.

Tom was left alone to his fancies. Now his nightmares included nightly visits from the ghosts of both his father and his grandfather. They shook their fists and demanded he deliver the final skull. As his mind became more unstable, he grew more and more determined to carry out his promise and so put his ghosts to rest. When he heard that a band of Indians had been seen in the neighborhood, Tom took up his rifle and set out on his horrible mission.

Shortly after this, a nearby settler heard a single shot from the direction of Tom's cabin. Hurrying to see what had happened, the man found the cabin silent and the door closed. He knocked and called out, but there was no answer. At last he pushed open the door and entered.

Staring blindly at him from the topmost shelf at the center of the far wall was the hundredth skull, a bullet hole through its forehead.

The head, which had been scalped, was Tom Quick's.

The Ogre's Arm

(Japan)

In Japan long ago there was a large plain, which was said to be haunted by an ogre. From time to time travelers crossing it would disappear, never to be heard from again. People in nearby villages whispered dreadful stories of how the missing folk had been lured away by the goblin and eaten.

One evening a brave knight named Watanabe rode onto the empty plain as a storm came on. Rain fell heavily and the wind howled like the wolves in the mountains. The weary knight was relieved when he spotted a clump of trees in the distance, and, through the trees, the glimmer of a lamp.

Hoping to find shelter for the night, Watanabe soon came to a miserable-looking little cottage. The bamboo fence was broken, and weeds and grass had pushed through the gaps. The paper screens covering the windows were full of holes. The old thatched roof sagged on posts that were bent with age.

The door was open. A young man, dressed as a farmer, looked up from his bowl of rice in surprise when Watanabe knocked on the doorpost.

"Good evening, sir," the knight said. "I beg you to let me take shelter for the night under your roof."

"Of course," said the farmer. "I can only offer you a poor welcome, but come in. I will make a fire to warm you."

He told the traveler to put his horse in the stable, which was as tumbledown as the house. When Watanabe had done so, he politely took off his boots (for he was in armor) and entered the hut. The younger man gave him a cup of tea, then said, "We will soon be out of wood. I must go and gather some more." Before he left, however, he cautioned the knight, "You must sit where you are, and not go near the back room."

"As you wish," said the knight, somewhat puzzled.

Then the farmer went away. Soon the remaining fire died out, and the only light came from a dim lantern. The farmer's warning not to look into the back room increasingly aroused Watanabe's curiosity and unease.

At last, deciding that he could take a look without his host knowing, Watanabe crept forward and pushed open the sliding door at the back of the room. What he saw froze the blood in his veins. The floor was littered with dead men's bones, while heaped in a corner, a stack of skulls reached to the ceiling.

Quickly Watanabe put his boots back on and hurried to the stable, for he had left his weapons with his horse.

But as soon as he entered the stable and reached for his sword, he became aware of someone standing behind him. At the same time the farmer's voice said, "My dear guest, why such haste to be away into the storm? Have you looked where you were warned not to look? And we had so little time to talk. Alas!"

With this, Watanabe's helmet was seized from the back. Quickly the knight put out his hand and groped around to

find out what held him from behind. He touched an
arm—but it was not human: It was covered with bristles
and as big as a tree trunk.

Watanabe wrenched free and spun around. He discovered that the farmer had taken on his true goblin shape.
He was taller than two men. His eyes flashed like sunlit
mirrors, his hair streamed out on all sides as though it
were made of living snakes, his mouth was filled with
bloodred fangs.

The ogre grabbed for him again, but Watanabe swung
his sword fiercely. There was a dreadful yell of pain, and
the ogre backed off. Then the knight attacked the ogre
with all his strength. At last the monster, who clearly was
better at deceiving travelers than fighting a war-hardened
soldier, took flight.

Watanabe pursued the ogre, but quickly lost the creature in the stormy darkness. Returning to the stable, the
knight stumbled upon something lying on the ground. It
was the ogre's arm, which the monster had lost in their
fight.

Wrapping it up, Watanabe rode home to Kyoto with the
arm as a trophy. When he showed it to his comrades, they
declared him a hero and gave him a great feast. Soon word
of his deed spread, and people came from far and wide,
hoping to see the ogre's arm.

But Watanabe knew the ogre was still alive and might try
to steal back his arm. So he had a box made of the stron-
gest wood, banded with iron. He refused to open it for
anyone. He left the box in his own room and never let it
out of his sight.

One evening soon after this, he had a visitor. He recognized the old woman at once: She had been his nurse

when he was a child. He greeted her warmly, though he thought it strange that she should come so late at night.

As they shared a friendly cup of tea, the old woman suddenly asked, "Master, the report of your brave fight with the ogre is so widely told that even your poor old nurse has heard of it. Is it really true that you cut off one of the ogre's arms? If you did, you are to be praised indeed."

"Yes," admitted Watanabe, "but I am ashamed that the monster escaped with only the loss of an arm!"

"Oh! There is nothing that can be compared to your courage! Please, let me see this arm," she begged.

"I am sorry," said Watanabe, "but I cannot. Ogres are very vengeful creatures. If I open the box for a moment, the ogre may suddenly appear to carry off his arm. So I never show it to anyone."

"Your caution is reasonable," said the old woman. "But I am your old nurse. Surely you will not refuse to show *me* the arm. Didn't I come rushing through the night to your door the moment I heard of your brave deed?"

Watanabe was troubled by her disappointed look. Still, he refused.

Then the old woman grew angry. "Do you suspect me of being a spy sent by the ogre?" she demanded.

"No, of course not," Watanabe answered, sighing. "You are my old nurse."

"Then do not deny this poor old woman her heart's wish," she pleaded. Tears began to roll down her cheeks.

Defeated, Watanabe said, "Very well. I will show you the ogre's arm. Come, follow me."

He led her to his own room. When he had carefully shut the door, Watanabe lifted the heavy lid on the iron-banded box in the corner of the room.

"Let me have a good look at it!" cried the woman joyfully. She came nearer and nearer, her face shining with eagerness.

Suddenly she plunged her hand into the box and seized the arm, roaring so that the room shook, "I have got my arm back!"

The nurse changed triumphantly into the towering figure of the frightful ogre. Watanabe, whose sword was always at his side, drew it from its sheath in a flash. But the ogre knew only too well the man's skill with a sword. He sprang to the ceiling and burst through the roof, vanishing into the night.

Though people continued to tell the story of Watanabe and the ogre's arm, the knight raged at the way the ogre had tricked him. In fury, he returned to the haunted plain to confront the monster. But the farmer's hut had fallen to ruins; wind and rain had ground the bones and skulls to dust.

Watanabe raised his sword and cried challenge after challenge to the unseen ogre. But his only answer was a sound like mocking laughter, so faint that it might have been nothing more than the wind stirring distant pines.

The Hairy Hands

(British Isles—England)

There is a road that stretches from Postbridge to Two Bridges, across the rugged and desolate landscape of Dartmoor. It is reportedly haunted. For years, pony carts would overturn into the ditch alongside the road. Horses would shy, throw their riders, and gallop off. In later years, bicyclists swore that their handlebars would be suddenly wrenched out of their control, sending them crashing. Cars and buses would skid—often causing fatal accidents.

Once, a young army officer was injured in a motorcycle crash. The shaken man insisted that, just a second before he had slammed into a stone wall, a pair of large, muscular, hairy hands had closed over his own, forcing his cycle off the road.

Some locals were convinced that the ghostly hands belonged to a highwayman who had held up coaches centuries before. As punishment the authorities had cut his hands off and thrown them away. "Not havin' a proper Christian burial," one person said, "them hands took on a life of their own."

When reporters got wind of this story, the mystery of the hairy hands became front-page news. Marjory Landis had followed the reports with interest. So when her husband,

Frederick, suggested they rent a camper and explore Dartmoor on their summer holiday, she tried to get him to change his mind. But her fear of the haunted road made him laugh. "Those stories are nothing but rubbish designed to sell newspapers," he insisted. "You can't take them seriously."

Still, she remained uneasy when they actually began their holiday. In Postbridge they arranged to rent the camper from a local agent. When she asked a clerk about the haunting, he simply shook his head and said, "The experts checked that whole stretch of road. They found the paving pitched too sharply to the sides. They repaired it, and that's ended most stories of hairy hands."

This made Marjory feel a bit better about their journey. But she grew apprehensive when Frederick decided to stop for the night about a mile west of the place where the two worst accidents had happened.

They had a light meal, then retired early. But Marjory awoke with a start in the chilly night. She sat up, her heart pounding. Through one of the camper's small windows, she could see moonlight shining on the ruins of an old mill. Though nothing seemed amiss, she felt a sense of menace, as though danger were creeping up on them.

In his bunk at the far end of the camper, Frederick slept soundly. But a sudden faint noise drew Marjory's attention to the window above her husband. There she saw something moving. For a moment it seemed like a large, pale spider. Then she realized that it was the fingers and palm of a very large hand. The moonlight showed many dark hairs on the joints and on the back of the hand. It was clawing its way up and up, toward the top of the window, which was open a little. The sound she had heard was the faintest scraping of fingernails on the glass.

"Frederick!" she called, but her husband did not stir. The horrible thing continued climbing. Now she could see that, beyond the wrist, there was nothing. It looked as though it had been cut cleanly off a body. She imagined the hand reaching the opening, scuttling through, dropping onto her sleeping husband's face.

Never taking her eyes off the horror, she hurried to Frederick. But even shaking him failed to rouse him.

The hairy hand was almost to the top. Frantically she slammed the window shut and bolted it. Frustrated, the fingers scrabbled back and forth, seeking a way in.

The hand sank slowly out of sight. But then she heard soft patterings along the wall. The window near her own bunk rattled. The danger wasn't gone. The thing was seeking another way in.

Not knowing what else to do, Marjory grabbed the Bible she kept beside her bed. She made the sign of the cross, then began reading aloud in a shaky voice.

Suddenly she heard a fist slammed against the wall near her head. Then again. The camper shook. She had the feeling that the thing was angered by her reading. While the unseen hand pounded away, she continued to read her Bible, though her voice grew weak and sometimes failed her.

And then, after one final blow, the assault stopped. She continued to read for several more minutes before pausing to listen. Her blood ran cold. A sound like fingernails scraping on the metal side of the trailer behind her was echoed by a second set of unseen nails scratching outside the opposite wall.

With a groan, Marjory realized that the reports had always spoken of *two* hands. She imagined the ghastly things hunting like a pair of small, lethal animals.

They were moving together now, one on either side of the camper, heading back toward the window over Frederick's bed.

Still holding the Bible, Marjory leaned over her husband, shaking him and shouting until she roused him. He seemed dazed, and angry with her for waking him so violently.

"Listen!" she cried. "Don't you hear them?"

"Hear what?" Frederick snapped. "There's nothing to hear."

The hands were silent.

Her husband was now fully awake and thoroughly angry. "You and those fool stories of yours!" he said. "Hairy hands. Ghosts. What rot!"

He pointed to the window. "There's nothing out there, Marjory. You get a grip; I'm going to make a cup of tea, since I'm awake now." He sat on the edge of the bunk to pull on his slippers.

Outside the window appeared the misty figure of a big man wearing a mask over his eyes, a plumed hat, and a loose shirt and doublet. He thrust his two bare, hairy fists through the windowpane. The spray of glass sent Frederick ducking with a cry. Behind him, the hairy hands grabbed for him.

Though Marjory had been cut by some bits of glass, she opened the Bible halfway, then slammed it closed on the outstretched fingers.

There was a sickening sizzling sound like frying sausages, and the smell of burning sulfur. Beneath its mask, the face of the ghostly highwayman twisted in pain and fear. Then the misty shape flew apart. The pages of the Bible thumped together a moment later as the hands vanished.

Neither Marjory nor her husband was hurt, except for some minor cuts from the glass. Frederick, whose back had been toward the hands and the ghostly figure, still groped for some "logical explanation." Then Marjory opened the Bible.

There, burned into the pages, was the clear impression of two big hands.

The Snow Husband

(Native American—Algonquin tribe)

In a northern village of the Algonquins dwelt a young woman so beautiful that many young men came to woo her. So lovely was she that she received the name Fairest.

Now, one of the young men who was most in love with her was named Elegant, because of his noble features and the rich beadwork on his clothing. One day he went to her father's lodge to ask Fairest if she would marry him.

But when he had poured out all his love to her, the maiden only laughed at him and rudely sent him away. To make things worse, she stood outside her father's lodge and repeated her refusal, shaming him in front of everyone.

Elegant, who was very sensitive, suffered terribly at being rejected and mocked so. His heartsickness soon turned into an illness of his whole body. He would not eat. He sat for hours staring at the ground, remembering Fairest's harsh words and the laughter of everyone who had heard them. He felt sad and disgraced. The kind words of family and friends did nothing to improve his spirits.

When his tribe was preparing to move to winter camp, he refused to leave with his family. At last the others could wait no longer, and they bade him sad farewell. He had grown so weak that they thought he would not live to see their return in the summer.

For a time, he lay shivering as the first snows began to fall. But at the very moment icy death seemed closest to him, Elegant found himself beginning to burn with the desire for revenge. He decided to punish Fairest for casting aside the love he had so honestly given her. He felt he had laid his heart at her feet, and she had treated it like a scrap not fit for dogs.

So Elegant appealed to his guardian spirit to help him. In a dream, the spirit came to him in the form of a wolf and told Elegant what he must do. As soon as the young man awoke, he ate a little pounded corn soaked in snow water for strength.

Then he did as the spirit had instructed. Going through the abandoned camp, he collected all the rags he could find. Tying animal bones together, he built a framework with two arms, two legs, and a dog's skull. The form stood as tall as himself. Over this he packed and sculpted snow into the figure of a man. He then clothed the snowman in the rags and tatters he had gathered. Lastly he decorated it with his own brilliant beads and bright feathers.

Then, saying the magic words the wolf spirit had taught him, he gave life to the figure, which now seemed the handsomest man the world had seen. "I name you Moowis," said Elegant. "You are my brother." Then he placed a bow and some arrows in the figure's hands.

Together, the pair set out for the tribe's winter camp. There the lordly appearance of Moowis made the young men jealous, but the young women felt their hearts go out to him. The chief of the tribe invited Moowis into his lodge and treated him as an honored guest. But Moowis did not approach the fire in the center of the lodge. He let others sit between him and the flames.

No one in the camp was as charmed by the noble-looking stranger as was Fairest. Her parents often invited Moowis to their lodge. Elegant watched all this with grim satisfaction. Soon news ran through the encampment that Moowis was to wed Fairest. Elegant was the first and loudest to express his wish for the couple's happiness.

Shortly after they were wed, Moowis told his wife, "I must go on a long journey."

When she asked him the reason, he only sighed.

"Let me come with you," she begged.

"Yes, this is how it must be," he said sadly.

Fairest was puzzled by his sadness. But she was so in love with him that she did not ask him any more questions. It was enough that they would be together.

They set out the next morning. Elegant watched them with joy and sorrow equally mixed in his heart. The road was rough and rugged. Still Moowis refused to say where they were going or why. Soon Fairest, whose feet were cut and bleeding, had a hard time keeping up with her stronger husband.

At first it had been bitterly cold, but now the warming spring sun was shining in all its strength. For a time, Fairest forgot her troubles and began to sing a happy little song.

But then she noticed a change in her husband. At first Moowis tried to keep in the shade to avoid the sun's rays. But the air grew warmer and warmer. Slowly the magical figure of snow dissolved and fell to pieces. His frenzied wife watched him become only rags soaked with snowmelt, the bony frame that had held the figure together, and scattered feathers and beads.

Fairest screamed his name over and over again. At last, exhausted with grief, she threw herself down beside the damp rags and tatters that had been her beloved. One last time she whispered, "Moowis," before she breathed her last.

So was Elegant avenged.

The Zimwi

(Africa—from the Swahili)

Once, some children went out to hunt for sea-shells on the shore. One, a girl named Mbodze, found a beautiful shell. Amid delicate ripples of brown and coral twined the shape of a python so yellow it seemed almost gold. Mbodze realized at once that the figure of the snake would make the shell a good-luck charm. Afraid to lose it, she laid it on a big round rock, to pick up on her way home. But she forgot the pretty shell until she, her sister, Matezi, and her brother, Nyange, started for home that evening. Suddenly remembering it, she asked the others to go back with her.

"No," said Matezi, "and you must not go back, either! I have heard that a *zimwi*—an ogre—comes to the beach at night."

"But the shell is so pretty," said Mbodze. "And it has the image of a golden python. Surely it will bring me good luck!"

Nyange said, "It will bring you bad luck if you go back for it after dark."

"The sun is not fully set," Mbodze said stubbornly. "I will be on my way home before it is truly night."

But for all her brave words, she was uneasy.

So Mbodze returned alone, singing to keep her courage up. When she reached the big stone, she met a young man with long hair, sitting beside a *nqoma,* big drum, with her shell in his hand.

"You sing so beautifully," said the man. "What do you want?"

"Please, sir, I want my shell, which you are holding."

"Of course," he said. "But you must sing again."

So Mbodze sang her song another time.

"So sweet," said the man. "But my hearing is not good. Come closer."

Mbodze did. At that moment, the young man turned into a *zimwi,* with two heads, two mouthfuls of fangs, and claws. He grabbed her with his long arms, and put Mbodze into the drum.

"Why have you done this?" the girl cried.

"Your sweet voice will be the voice of my drum," he said. "When I play for people, they will reward me with food."

So he set off. At each village, the monster turned himself into a young man. Then he went to the meeting place and announced he would play his wondrous drum in return for chickens and yams.

He beat the drum, and the imprisoned Mbodze sang along. Everyone was delighted. The ogre was paid with a great deal of food, but he gave just enough to the girl to keep her alive. Though she tried and tried, she could not free herself from the drum.

In time, they came to Mbodze's home village. Her parents were mourning the loss of their child and did not come to hear the *zimwi* play his singing drum. But Mbodze's sister and brother, Matezi and Nyange, did. Right away the children recognized their sister's voice. They ran and told their parents.

When the grown-ups heard, they guessed what had hap-

pened. But they could not confront the *zimwi*. In his true shape, the monster was strong, and could easily kill them or run away with the drum.

So Mbodze's parents invited the *zimwi* to their house. There they gave him so much food that the family had to borrow more from their neighbors. Still the hungry creature ate, until his stomach grew almost as big as the drum he leaned against. When he could not eat another bite, he fell asleep.

Quickly her parents opened the drum and released Mbodze, hugged her quietly, then hid her with her brother and sister in a neighbor's hut. Next they put a poisonous snake and a swarm of bees and some biting ants inside the drum. Then they closed it up again. Lastly they shook the *zimwi* awake. "Drummer, wake up!" they said. "Some strangers have come who want to hear your music."

The *zimwi* took his drum to the meeting place and began to beat it. But the voice inside was silent. He went on beating it, but nothing happened. He began to shout and pound more loudly on the drum. The silence made him angrier. At last, careless of the watching villagers, he pulled off the drumskin.

Instantly the bees and biting ants swarmed over him, stinging him until he stumbled over the drum. Then the deadly snake shot out and bit him, and the monster died. When he was dead, he returned to his true, horrible shape. Then the ground drank him down as though he were made of water.

On the spot where the *zimwi* had died, there soon sprang up a pumpkin vine. It bore a single pumpkin of amazing size. Each day it grew bigger and bigger. Soon it was as big as the chief's hut.

While the pumpkin grew, a strange thing happened. The people of the village began to disappear. Each night more vanished. The chief posted guards to watch over the village at night, but they were gone the next morning.

People began to flee the village in fear. Meanwhile the pumpkin had grown as wide as twenty elephants side by side and as tall as a palm tree.

When all their neighbors had left, Mbodze's parents made plans to move to another village. But on the last night, Mbodze was awakened by a soft voice that called, "Come out. See how fine the pumpkin looks in the moonlight."

Mbodze rose from her bedding. To her surprise, she saw her mother, father, sister, and brother going out into the night.

Again the voice called, "Come out." But the girl hesitated. When she could resist no longer, she walked toward the huge pumpkin, glowing in the moonlight.

Because she had waited, she was behind the others. She saw them go up to the pumpkin. On its smooth, round side, a huge mouth appeared. As her family went forward like sleepwalkers, the pumpkin swallowed them one by one.

Then the mouth said to Mbodze, "Oh-ho! Here is the little voice of my drum. Come closer! You won't escape me again."

The girl realized that the pumpkin was the *zimwi*, returned in this new shape. Frightened, she ran to her hut even as the *zimwi* roared, "Come back!"

She felt her body obeying the ogre's awful magic. But as she was turning to go, she snatched up her father's war ax.

Holding this behind her back, she walked to the pumpkin and let it swallow her up.

Inside was a vast, damp, dark space. All around her, the girl could hear the voices of adults and children crying and calling out to one another. She heard the voices of her family.

Stretching out her hand, she felt the curved inside of the pumpkin. Without hesitating, Mbodze swung her ax again and again. Soon she had chopped a hole in the side of the pumpkin. As moonlight streamed in through the hole, the *zimwi* began to shake and roar in pain. But the girl kept chopping. When the hole was big enough, she led all the trapped people out.

Still she chopped at the pumpkin, which was too weak to make any more magic. Then all the villagers took knives and axes and hacked the pumpkin to bits. Finally they burned the pieces to ashes and scattered them. Then they praised Mbodze for her courage. And the village was never bothered by the *zimwi* again.

Witchbirds

(France)

Once upon a time, in Provence, in the south of France, there were three witches—daughter, mother, and grandmother—who lived together in a cottage near a small village. They kept to themselves, and the villagers kept away out of fear. From time to time, though, someone would ask the weird women for a healing potion or a love charm in return for a bushel of corn or a basket of eggs.

But people whispered that the women worked far stronger magic in secret, often under cover of night. Some claimed they could turn themselves into cats or rabbits or even night birds. In this last form, they would fly to distant meetings of their sisters, away in the woods or on mountaintops or across the sea.

It was these last stories that interested the boy Léonce. But when he asked his mother, "Can such a thing be?" she told him, "True or not, it's no business of yours."

When he asked, "Can witches fly?" his mother scolded him and forbade him to bring up the subject again. When he asked the other people in the village, they warned him, "You'll bring bad luck on yourself if you even talk of such things."

But Léonce could only imagine how wonderful it would be to soar on wings above town and wood, lake and hill.

He dreamed of traveling to the ends of the earth on magic wings and seeing all the wonders of the world.

At last he got up nerve enough to go to the witches' cottage. The grandmother answered his knock. "Why are you here?" she asked impatiently.

Léonce explained, "I want to learn the secret of night-flying. In return, I would work for you."

The woman's face grew hard. "Off with you, boy! You're a fool to even think such a thing." And she slammed the door.

Anger made Léonce even more determined to get what he wanted, one way or another. He decided to spy on the women to see if he could learn their secret.

That very night, shortly before midnight, he crept up to the cottage window. Peeping in, Léonce saw that the main room was dimly lit by the glowing embers in the hearth. The grandmother and the mother stood beside the fire-place, while the daughter took a jar of ointment from a small cabinet. Dipping their fingers in, the women touched their heads and hands and shoes with the oint-ment. Each time they cried out *"Supra fueillo,"* which meant "above the foliage" or "over the leaves."

As soon as they had finished this business, they suddenly became owls. Hooting loudly, they flew up the chimney. From his hiding place, Léonce saw the three witchbirds fly across the face of the moon. Then they vanished into the night.

Eagerly the boy pried open the window. Thinking only of how exciting it would be to see the world from above, he grabbed the jar that sat atop the cabinet. His hand shaking with excitement, he dipped his fingers into the ointment and touched himself with it as the women had done. But in his haste, he did not remember the exact words they had used. Instead of crying *"Supra fueillo,"* he said *"Souto fueillo,"* which meant "under the foliage" or "beneath the leaves."

Scarcely had Léonce shouted *"Souto fueillo"* for the last time when he was transformed into an owl. Then he flew directly toward the chimney. But instead of soaring up the flue, he knocked against the grate that held smoldering green wood to which a few leaves clung.

Stunned and burned, he lay in the ashes a moment. Then, deciding the accident had happened because he was not used to the shape and movements of a bird, he tried again. This time, afraid of burning himself again, he flew out the window, which he had left open.

But when Léonce reached the open country, he began to have more problems. Where the fields were bare, he found he could fly as easily as an ordinary owl. But as soon as he came to a hedge or thicket, he was forced to pass through it instead of flying above it. Every branch, twig, and thorn hit and stung him like a whip.

Léonce wished he could stop flying: Every moment brought fresh pain. But it was impossible to stop; some power kept his wings beating and forced him straight ahead. However much he tried, he could not avoid the bushes and trees that lay in his path. The words *"souto fueillo"*—"under the leaves"—were making him fly, crawl, bite, and claw his way beneath the leaves of every growing plant.

He was bruised and wounded all over. He felt near death. Ahead he saw a bramble thicket bristling with long, cruel thorns. The magic forced him to half fly, half hobble, toward the fatal hedge. He knew he would be torn to pieces before he was compelled halfway through. In his heart, he prayed for a quick end.

But inches short of the nearest thorns, Léonce heard a cock crow. The first hint of dawn tinted the sky. The night had ended, and the night's magic ended, too. Léonce fell heavily to the ground. He found himself a boy again. His clothes were in tatters; he was bruised and bleeding and smarting from a hundred deep scratches; but he was alive! And for this he said a prayer of thanksgiving.

Limping and dizzy, he made his painful way home. There his mother put him to bed and nursed him. But when she asked what had happened, he only said that he had gotten lost in the woods. And when his wounds had healed, Léonce found he was also cured of any wish to learn the secret of the witchbirds.

Dangerous Hill

(British Isles—England)

An easy drive south from London, along the coast, will bring a traveler to a secluded spot where nature's beauty is unspoiled. Here the summer air is rich with the scent of pine trees, and the hills are alive with wildflowers.

In this lovely setting, a lonely, silent house of white stone, its windows shuttered, sits atop a hill. Above the bright swirls of flowers and fragrant woods, it squats and broods over the landscape. House and slope together are called Dangerous Hill. There are many stories to explain the name; here is one.

In the 1930s, a young woman named Tanith Moore married William Braden. They decided to honeymoon for a month in a house on the south coast. Tanith had heard of an attractive, fully furnished house just fifty miles from London.

"It will be perfect," she told William. "It has a tennis court and a swimming pool—plus masses of flowers. I so love flowers!"

William, eager to please, said, "And we'll be close enough to drive up to London for plays and visiting friends."

Tanith turned serious for a moment. "The place has a

funny name, though: Dangerous Hill. At least, that's what it's called on the rental agreement. The real estate agent didn't want to talk about it. She said it was because the road to the top of the hill has dangerous curves." Now she sounded quite worried. "You *have* got that new sports car, darling. And you *do* drive fast."

"Don't be silly!" her husband said. "The car handles beautifully. Dangerous Hill has more than met its match."

Indeed, William's car took the steep, tree-lined hill road as gracefully and easily as a bird in flight.

The place was a dream—gleaming white in the sunlight, flowers everywhere. The caretaker, who lived in the nearby town, met them and gave them the keys. Tanith and William explored the house and gardens with delight. At last they sat down to rest on a bench by a pool dotted with water lilies.

Suddenly they saw a tall woman, dressed in an old-fashioned black gown, approaching. They were both startled because the garden and the hillside below had seemed empty a moment before. The woman was handsome, but sad-faced. And there was something odd about her that William could not quite put his finger on.

"What brings you here?" she asked. Her voice was faint, as though it came from far away.

"We're on our honeymoon," said Tanith. "This house is the perfect place. We're going to be very happy here."

"Others thought so, too," the woman said. *"The hill did not allow them to be happy."*

"What are you talking about?" asked William. He was annoyed that the woman's gloomy appearance and words were spoiling their first day at the house.

"I bought the house years ago," she said, "although I

was told that the hill belongs to powers as old as time. These forces don't like being disturbed. But the place was so beautiful, I would not listen."

The strange woman turned to the young couple. "*You must listen: Don't stay here. Go home. Forget this place. Remember the other two.*"

"Who were the other two?" asked Tanith.

All at once they heard a church bell toll in the distance.

"That is the passing bell!" said the woman. "*Be warned! The hill must have its sacrifice!*"

William was really angry now. But the woman smiled a curious, twisted smile. And then she was gone. She disappeared as quickly as she had come. And William realized what had struck him as odd about her: Though there was sunlight everywhere, *she had thrown no shadow.*

Tanith shivered as she asked, "Was she a ghost? What did she mean by 'powers'? What powers? This is all so strange! I don't know if I want to stay here."

"We haven't unpacked the car," said William, who was just as shaken as his wife. "We'll leave now. I'll phone the agent when we get back to London. Say we've changed our minds."

Leaving the keys in the hallway, they hurried to the car. From somewhere came the sound of laughter, though neither the caretaker nor anyone else was in sight. To Tanith, the hill suddenly looked very steep. A sign they hadn't noticed before warned, DANGEROUS HILL.

"Be careful, William," Tanith begged.

But the car fairly flew down the hillside, taking the dangerous curves as smoothly as it had when climbing them. Tanith breathed more easily when they rounded the last curve and reached the bottom of the hill. From here the road stretched flat and straight ahead. But the air seemed alive with voices as steady and meaningless as crickets' humming. And somewhere the passing bell tolled again.

Then, dead ahead, a big truck shot out of a hidden side road. There was no time to brake. William's sports car hit the truck with a sickening grinding noise.

William was killed instantly. Tanith, though badly injured, recovered. In the days that followed, she tried to make sense of the tragedy. There seemed so many bits and pieces to fit together in the puzzle. She often talked to people who lived near Dangerous Hill, though she could not go back there. Even the sight of the place—the slopes covered with flowers, the house shimmering in the sunlight—chilled her to the bone.

Then, one day, she met an old man who had lived his whole life near there. When he heard her story, he nodded and said, "Your husband was a sacrifice to the Things that own Dangerous Hill. The ghost—oh yes! she was certainly a ghost; she's been dead many years—was right to warn you. It's a pity her warning came too late."

"Then you know who she was?" asked Tanith.

"Yes," said the old man. "She had an only son, very much like your William, I imagine. He was engaged to a pretty girl like you. The young people were killed in a car crash on Dangerous Hill. The poor mother died of a broken heart soon after. All three are buried in the churchyard nearby. Perhaps the sound of the church's passing bell was another warning sent too late."

The Witch's Head

(El Salvador)

$\mathbf{A}$ young farmer named Luís took a cartload of fresh fruit to market one day. As he sat in the plaza with his goods spread out on a blanket, a lovely young woman, a stranger, stopped to look over his wares. Then she picked up a ripe *zapote*. Smiling, she bit into the juicy apple-shaped fruit. "Ah! Sweet *zapote*!" she cried. "It is my favorite fruit, but I have never tasted one half as sweet."

They began talking, and Luís learned that she had come to live with an elderly aunt. The farmer was captivated by the charming young woman, and began to call on her. Soon they were married.

Not long after the wedding, a witch began to trouble the neighborhood. The hag came by night. Jewels and other valuables would disappear. Food would be eaten. Unfortunate watchdogs or homeowners who discovered the witch at her business were found bitten to death.

No one knew what she looked like, though one or two people claimed to have seen a ghostly form, with dark hair streaming behind it, flying beneath the stars just before dawn. Witnesses would cross themselves, and pray that the sight didn't prove a curse.

Luís grew worried that the creature might come to his house and harm his wife. But when he told her his fears, she laughed. "That mischief-maker will never bother us," she said.

Her husband, however, decided she was merely acting brave so that he wouldn't worry. Luís did not tell her that he planned to keep watch all through the night. Later, while his wife slept in her bed, he only pretended to sleep. In the dark, he kept his eyes and ears open for the slightest movement or sound that would reveal the coming of the witch.

To his amazement, Luís saw his wife get up in the middle of the night. He was about to call to her when her actions stopped him. Moving silently, she put two cushions under her covers. Then she moved her hands in a curious pattern over the bed. She whispered words he could not hear. To his horror, the bedclothes began to rise and fall gently as if his wife were still asleep.

In the main room, she swung herself up to the ceiling beams, then dropped straightaway to the floor, where her body lay headless. But her head—which now had the features of a withered, sharp-toothed old woman—floated above the body a moment. Then it vanished through the door, which opened and closed by itself. Paralyzed with fright, the farmer spent the next hours praying.

Before cockcrow, the door swung open. For a moment Luís saw his wife, with her witch's face, standing there. Her dark hair trailed down over a form as clear and colorless as glass. Then, from the neck down, the body faded away like smoke in the breeze. All that was left was the hideous head, which floated over and rejoined the body lying on the floor. The moment she was whole again, her face became as lovely as before. The woman stood up. Her husband saw his wife return to bed, rearrange her bedclothes, and fall asleep as the sun was beginning to rise.

Later that day, the terrified farmer went to an old man who was supposed to know a thing or two about witches. "What am I to do?" he asked when he had told the fellow of his wife's secret.

"When your wife goes out to make mischief," the old man said, "let her body lie where it is. But put a heap of hot ashes on the spot where the head belongs."

That night the farmer did as he was told. Then he hid himself in the loft. When the head returned, it could not attach itself to its body. Its face twisting in rage, the head cried, "How have you dared to do this, you miserable man?" Then it flew about the room screaming and gnashing its razor-sharp teeth.

The farmer, crouching in the loft, kept silent. But his foot slipped, making a noise. The head flew up and faced him. "Cruel husband," it said, "you have shut me away from my own body forever. Now you will have to share your body with me."

So the awful head settled on his shoulder and stuck fast. The man wept at his misfortune. He knew he could never rid himself of a witch who had fastened on his body this way.

In despair, the man ran into the woods beyond his farm. All the while, the witch's head, which had little power during the day, dozed. As the man wandered about, he found himself at the base of a gigantic *zapote* tree. High above, the *zapotes* were just beginning to ripen.

Suddenly he had an idea. Gently he began to stroke the head. "Poor thing," he said soothingly, "you are so tired. Sleep, sleep in the warm sun." Then he pointed up to the ripening fruit. "Look! There are *zapotes*. Wouldn't you like some to eat? I know how fond you are of them."

"Let me sleep," the head complained.

"Please sleep while I fetch you some *zapotes,*" the man said, spreading his serape on the ground.

"Yes," the head murmured. "Sweet *zapotes.*"

Then it said, "I will rest. But do not try to escape. I will be waiting." The head let the farmer lift it down from his shoulder and gently place it on the serape. Then the farmer climbed the tree and got hold of some green *zapotes.* He hurled them with all his force at the head.

"*Traitor!*" screeched the head. "Come down so that I can punish you!" It began to jump about, snapping its teeth and growling. But the man continued to pelt the head with hard green fruit.

Looking about for a way to escape, the head spotted a deer. Confused by the shouting, the deer ran right past the tree. With its last bit of strength, the head jumped high enough to settle on the back of the animal. The terrified deer charged into the wood while the head screamed and its hair whipped about in the wind, driving the animal to madness. So it was that the deer plunged over a cliff into a deep valley.

A long time after this, some hunters found the dusty bones of what seemed to be a deer with two skulls, the second one human. Shuddering, they ran from the place. Nor would they ever go near the valley again.

Dinkins Is Dead

(United States—South Carolina)

Wadmalaw Island is one of the Sea Islands just off the South Carolina coast. Many years ago, a man named Theodore Dinkins lived there. He was so opinionated and stubborn, no one could convince him of anything.

He had lived many years, and so he grew old. He, however, did not believe it. "Old?" he said angrily. "Me? I'm not old."

Yet he began to look old and to be old, to go to bed early and get up late, to be well one day and ill the next. But the worse he grew, the better he said he felt.

His doctor, his lawyer, and his minister came to see him. They told him he was dying; they wanted to help him make out his will; they wanted to help him make his peace with the Lord.

"I am not dying!" he shouted, and sent them away. But he really was dying.

When he was dead, the undertaker laid him out in his coffin. The sexton tolled the bell. The preacher read the burial service. His widow wept. All his friends said, "Death has convinced him, even if nothing else could."

But death had not.

The next morning a friend from another town rode by the graveyard. He saw Dinkins sitting on the fence, looking a little odd but nothing too strange. "Hello, Tom!" Old Dinkins called.

"This is a surprise," said the neighbor. "I heard you were at death's door. To tell the truth, I heard you were dead and buried."

"Do I look dead?" asked Dinkins.

"We-ell . . ." The neighbor hesitated. There was something about the old man's look that bothered him.

"We-ell yourself!" Dinkins bellowed. "I'm not dead, and any fool can see I'm not buried."

"Yes," said the neighbor, riding on to avoid an argument.

Soon it began to rain. A traveling man from town came by. He was startled when a voice from the graveyard called, "Hello!" Reining in his horse, the traveler peered through the downpour. He saw an old man sitting on the graveyard fence. He couldn't say what it was, exactly, but the look of the old man was . . . strange. "How do?" the traveler asked.

"Fine enough," said the old man. "Coming from town?"

"Yes, sir."

"What's the news?"

"Old Man Dinkins is dead."

" 'Tain't so."

"But, sir," said the traveler, angry that the old man had contradicted him, "I heard it from the widow Dinkins herself."

"Clementina Dinkins?" said the old man. "Why, she never got anything right in her life."

"Still and all, sir, you must admit she should know if her own husband is dead or not."

"Sure she *ought* to," said the old man, "but she evidently don't."

"How come you know better?" the man challenged.

" 'Cause I'm Theodore Dinkins."

"The devil you are!" cried the traveling man, and he rode off. At the crossroads store he stopped and said, "There's an old fool sitting on the graveyard fence who says he's Theodore Dinkins."

"Can't be," said the store owner. "Dinkins is dead."

Things went on this way, week after week, month after month. Everyone knew that Dinkins was dead. But Theodore Dinkins sat on the graveyard fence and said he was not; he grew mighty angry if anyone contradicted him. And he was looking worse and worse.

What was to be done? The town had buried him once.

"Bury him again," said Clementina Dinkins, who was mild but firm. So they buried him again, ignoring all his protests. But this time they put above his grave a marble headstone that read:

Here Rests the Body of
Theodore Dinkins
A Highly Respected Native of
Wadmalaw Island
Who Departed This Life on
the Seventeenth Day of January, 1853,
in the Ninety-first Year of His Age.

When Theodore read that inscription on his own tombstone, he was at last persuaded. It was the only time he was ever known to be convinced by evidence or argument. In any case, he hasn't yelled at anybody from the graveyard fence since then.

Old Nan's Ghost

(British Isles—England)

One night a tinker was hurrying along the road to Stokesley. Suddenly a wild-haired old woman, wrapped in a black shawl, appeared out of the dark in front of his cart. With a curse, the man reined in his horse before he ran the woman down.

"Stand aside!" the man ordered as the horse reared and whinnied. Peering closer, he recognized the wrinkled face of Old Nan, who wandered the moors. It was rumored that she was a witch. To the tinker she had never seemed more than a half-mad beggar.

Silently the woman reached up and took the bridle. At her touch, the nervous horse grew calm. Then she led the animal along a rough track that branched off from the main road. The tinker tugged at the reins, but the horse plodded on, ignoring all but the old woman's controlling hand.

Furious at being led astray, the tinker shouted at the woman and cracked his whip above her head. But the hunched figure who held the bridle just shuffled on, unbothered. The spellbound horse followed.

At last they halted where the path ended, at the foot of a hill. The old woman pointed to the mouth of a cave, partly hidden by brush. She beckoned to the tinker. As though he was under her spell, he unhitched the lantern from his cart and came closer. At her silent urging, he went inside.

The place smelled of earth and decay. Looking around, the man found a drawstring pouch of flannel tucked into a rocky niche. The bag was filled with silver charms and jeweled rings and golden coins. The tinker could not imagine how the old woman, so aged and ragged, had come by such treasure.

Suddenly Old Nan's ghostly voice echoed in the cavern: "It's for her . . . for her."

Under other circumstances the man would have trembled with fear. But greed for the newfound fortune crowded out all other thoughts.

Nan's voice continued. "I have a niece, a sweet, generous girl, who lives in Northallerton. But she is very poor. Take this pouch to her and tell her to buy fine clothes and happiness. Tell her this is the gift of Old Nan. It is her earthly reward. You may keep two gold pieces for your help—that is your reward. The child's name is Anne Compton. Will you give her Old Nan's gift?"

"I will," the tinker promised.

There was only silence after this. The shadowed figure of the old woman had disappeared from the mouth of the cave.

When he reached Stokesley, the tinker learned that Nan had died upon the moors some weeks before. Though he guessed that he had met her ghost, this did not prevent him from keeping Old Nan's riches for himself. He prospered and became a wealthy merchant in Stokesley. Never once did he give a thought to the old woman's niece.

Often, in his dreams, Old Nan returned to haunt him. Each time she seemed more ghastly: As her bones were moldering out on the moors, so her ghost seemed to be rotting, too. He would dream himself back in the hidden cavern. There the aged, shawl-clad bundle of rotting flesh and bones would confront him.

"Will you give my niece her earthly reward?" the horror would ask.

"I will not," he would answer, pleased at his dream-courage. Then he would awaken with a start, and for a few moments he would still hear Old Nan's question. But he would turn over and fall asleep, assuring himself that the hag had been dead and gone for many years.

Sometimes he thought he caught a glimpse of a dark figure shambling along behind him in town. "Will you give my niece her earthly reward?" he once fancied she asked. But when he turned, he saw nothing. "I will *not!*" he said aloud, dismissing it all.

At last, in a dream or in the street, her accusing voice faded to a whisper, then a sigh. He imagined her bones, picked clean, scattered across the Yorkshire hills and moors—barely strong enough a link to bind a ghost to the earth.

One last time she came to him while he was asleep. But her voice was weak. The dreaming man strode boldly across a moor, following the voice to its source: a sheltered space in a circle of tall rocks. Yellowing bones and bits of black cloth lay at the center of the ring.

"Will you give my niece, now grown an old woman and hungry, her earthly reward?" The voice issued from between the unmoving jaws of the yellowed skull at his dream-feet.

"I will not," said the rich man, sure that Nan's ghost was fading as her bones turned to dust. He kicked the skull aside; it rolled silently into the shadows. He woke up feeling pleased with himself.

One evening soon after this, the merchant was riding home on his fine new horse. Dusk was falling as he passed a rough track leading off the road. Something startled his horse and spurred it to a gallop, as though it were fleeing some terrifying presence. A figure leapt out of the dark and onto the horse just behind the merchant.

The man lashed with his whip at the thing that had grabbed him from behind. His nose was filled with the odor of rotten meat and decaying weeds and wet earth. Something made of old bones and mud and moor wrack, wearing an old shawl stained green with mold and slime, locked a dank, stinking arm across his throat.

"Will you give my niece her earthly reward?" demanded the specter in a gurgle.

"I will!" cried the tinker-turned-merchant.

"Too late!" the thing burbled. "She has gone to heaven today. Now you shall have *your* earthly reward!"

A farmer the horse passed on the road reported that he saw the merchant trying to escape the clutches of something clinging to his shoulders. All the time, the man was screaming out, *"I will, I will, I will!"*

"I would swear it was an old woman," the farmer said. "She was wrapped in a wretched black shawl, and her hair was blowing wild in the wind!"

When the runaway horse reached the village, it was foaming and panting with exhaustion. The merchant's corpse lay slouched over the saddle, his legs tangled in the stirrups. When they lowered the man's body to the ground, they found that his nostrils and mouth were clogged with mud. A piece of moldy black cloth was twisted tightly around his throat, and two gold pieces had been jammed into his eye sockets.

The Interrupted Wedding

(Norway)

It was late in summer, and most of the cattle had been driven from the high pastures to the meadows near town. But one young woman, Elli, remained behind in the hills to herd her cows through the last warm days of the year. Her friends had warned her against staying alone for fear that the *huldre* folk, the fairies who lived in the hills, might cause her harm. But she assured them, "I'm not worried. The hill people have never bothered me or my cows." People knew better than to argue with her: Elli was as strong-willed as she was pretty.

At night she slept in a little hut high on the moor, with her dog, Rapp, as company. But her loneliness didn't bother her; her mind was filled with thoughts of her upcoming wedding to handsome Olav.

Elli had just finished dinner, and the last rays of the sun had faded from the mountains, when there came a knock at the door. At first she was startled. But when she peeked out, she recognized Olav standing there. Delighted, she threw open the door.

"I thought you had to stay in the valley this week to help your father get the house ready for winter," she said. "How did you get away?"

"I was so lonely," he answered, "I thought we should get married tonight."

She was surprised at this. She was more surprised to see that a great number of folk had come with him. In the light of the full moon, she recognized Olav's father, as well as many friends and neighbors from the village. Tied nearby were the dark horses the company had ridden.

Suddenly her dog, Rapp, began to growl and snap. Elli scolded him, but Rapp only grew more frantic. Then the dog ran off into the night. "Good riddance!" said Olav. "Quick, now! Will you marry me on the spot?"

Feeling a bit strange but loving Olav very much, Elli cried, "Yes! If it's what you want."

Some of the women had brought a bridal gown and a crown of flowers for her to wear. While they dressed her and put rings on her fingers, others set out long tables laden with the finest foods. It was a wonder to Elli that they had carried so much all the way up from the village.

Soon she was sitting beside Olav, being toasted by his father. Then the priest stepped forward to marry them.

They had just reached the point where she would say the words that would make them man and wife when a rider came charging in, scattering the guests. To Elli's amazement, it was Olav's double. In puzzlement, she looked into the face of the bridegroom standing beside her. His handsome features were distorted with rage.

The rider raised his rifle and fired a bullet over the heads of the crowd. Elli screamed and clutched at Olav— but the man beside her was no longer Olav. He was not even a man! She realized that she had almost married herself to a *huldre* being. All around, the other guests had vanished, and she was surrounded by a throng of *huldre* folk. Their skin was blue; each had a long, ropelike cow's tail. The fine food on the tables had turned into moss and toadstools and cow dung.

Then the real Olav reached down, gathered up Elli, placed his sweetheart on the saddle in front of him, and spurred his horse away. Behind them, the angry *huldre* folk mounted their own dark horses and gave chase. They rode hard. But Olav suddenly wheeled his mount. He reloaded his rifle. In the moonlight, Elli saw that his bullets were silver. This was what had broken the spell the *huldre* folk had cast to make things appear as they were not.

Olav fired over the heads of the advancing dark riders. Instantly they fled in all directions. Then Olav and Elli galloped over field and stream until they had left their pursuers far behind.

They continued until they saw the house that belonged to Olav's father ahead, and the lights of the town beyond.

"We're safe at last!" the young man cried, hugging Elli in relief.

"But how did you know to come for me?" she asked.

"Your dog came to our house and whined and barked until I knew something was amiss."

"Good Rapp," said Elli. "Only a few minutes more and I would have been a *huldre* wife." She shivered at the thought. "But everything is right again," she said with a smile.

Then they saw Olav's father's house burst into flames, while the laughter of countless voices swept down on the wind from the hills.

The Mulombe

(Africa—Zimbabwe)

There was once a wicked man who was very poor. He was jealous of his uncles and cousins, who had herds of cattle and fields of yams, plantains, and bananas, and households with many servants. He wanted to make their wealth his own. So he went to a wizard who could make a *mulombe,* a magical, deadly creature that can kill a man's enemies.

He traveled with his only servant, Mbizo, an orphan boy, who was paid with scraps and beatings. When they reached the wizard's hut in a distant grove, the man told Mbizo, "Stay outside and wait for me. What goes on inside is not for you to know."

Mbizo, being curious, slipped around the side of the hut and peeped through a crack. He saw his master sitting across a small fire from the wizard, who wore many necklaces and held a walking stick carved with figures of snakes and birds and fish.

"What will you give me if I make a *mulombe?*" asked the sorcerer.

To the boy's astonishment, his master promised many head of cattle and bushels of yams. The man had no such wealth—how would he pay? And what was a *mulombe?* Mbizo wondered.

The wizard accepted the promised payment. Then he

rose and took medicines from pots and jars. These he put on a piece of bark and mixed with water. Next he took some grass and braided it into a plait about eighteen inches long and one inch wide. He placed this on a mat between the man and himself.

Then the sorcerer nicked the man's forehead and drew a drop of blood. He added this to the medicine on the piece of bark. He gave a bit to the man to eat; then he sprinkled the rest over the braid of grass three times.

The first sprinkling turned the braid ashy white. The second turned it into a pale snake. At the third sprinkling, the snake's head turned into the image of the man. There was even a tiny mark on his doll-like forehead that was the same as the mark where the wizard had drawn blood.

Mbizo, watching, was shivering with excitement.

The *mulombe* reared itself up on its tail and spoke to the man, saying, "You know me and recognize me?"

"Yes," said the man.

"You see that your face and mine are the same?" As it spoke, a snake's forked tongue darted between the human lips.

"I see that," the man answered.

Then the wizard placed the creature in a small basket and handed it to the man, saying, "This is the *mulombe* that you asked me for. Take it and tend it carefully. Keep it hidden wherever you wish. It will always be with you now. So long as you treat it well, you will not die—until all your relatives are dead."

As the man rose, Mbizo hurried away from the hut. A moment later his master emerged, carrying the little basket. On their return journey, it was all the boy could do not to keep staring at the grass basket.

When they returned to the village, the man told Mbizo

to sweep his hut. Then he went away; when he returned, he no longer had the basket. The boy guessed he had hidden the *mulombe*.

Soon after this, the man's uncle died. And his uncle's sons. All died without a mark upon them. Much of their wealth fell to the wicked man. Over the next weeks and months, more of the man's kin died, and their lands and cattle became his. He built a bigger hut and hired more servants. All around, the village mourned the passing of so many good people. Mbizo's master made a great show of mourning, also; but his sharp-eyed little servant saw how quickly his sad look gave way to one of triumph when he thought no one was looking.

Surely, Mbizo reasoned, the *mulombe* is the cause of all these deaths. But he was afraid to betray the man, for fear the *mulombe* would come after him.

Still, Mbizo tried to find out where his master had hidden the creature. When he could, he would follow his master in the hope of discovering something. Early one morning he trailed the man to a distant stretch of river. The man halted and gave a short whistle. Up from the river reeds rose the *mulombe*.

"You came to me in my dream last night," the man said.

"I want a person to kill," the *mulombe* whispered. "Give me the name of a person whose life force I may eat."

"All my relatives are dead," the man protested.

"If you do not name a person," the snake with a human head said, "I will become sick, and so will you. If I die, so will you. That is the bond between us. *Give me a name.*"

In horror, Mbizo heard the man say, "Mbizo. The boy is of little use to me."

"I will take him tonight," said the *mulombe*.

Mbizo fled, terrified, back to the village. What could he do? Even if he ran away, he was sure the magical creature would find him and slay him. How could one escape or fight a magical being? he asked himself. His only hope would be magic of his own.

So he went to the diviner to ask his advice. The man cast a handful of small animal bones several times, reading secrets in the patterns the bones made. Then he said to Mbizo, "Yours must be the hand that slays the *mulombe,* since you are his intended victim. Take this bow and poisoned arrow. You must use this to kill the thing. If you fail, you are lost."

Then the diviner summoned five strong men to accompany him and Mbizo to the riverbank. As they were leaving the village, they were seen by the boy's master. He looked at the group curiously, then continued on his way.

Near the reedy riverbank, the diviner took some medicine he had prepared and sprinkled it on the ground and among the reeds. Suddenly the ground began to rumble and the surface of the river began to churn. The water rose from the riverbed until Mbizo, his bow and poisoned arrow at the ready, and the others were thigh-deep. Fish and crabs struggled out of the water onto the land.

Suddenly the *mulombe* rose up on its tail. It hissed at Mbizo. The boy tried to steady his hand; then he released the arrow. But his trembling fingers betrayed him, and the arrow only nicked the creature.

There was a shout from the jungle's edge; Mbizo's master was charging down the bank. At that moment, the *mulombe* began to writhe and hiss in pain, for the arrow's nick had fatally poisoned it.

The *mulombe* lunged at Mbizo, then fell, curling and uncurling its length in the mud. The moment it collapsed, the boy's master underwent a horrifying change. His arms were drawn to his sides as if by invisible threads; they melted like wax into the man's body. The body, grown pale, began to stretch and narrow, while the man screamed as his bones and insides were pulled into a serpent shape. His bellows became hissing; his tongue, split at the end, darted serpentlike between still-human lips.

Then, like the *mulombe,* he fell writhing into the mud. Master and *mulombe* twisted among the reeds, churning the red clay of the riverbank and the stream itself into a blood-colored mess. Suddenly the *mulombe* shuddered a last time, grew rigid, then sank from sight. A moment later the second *mulombe,* which had once been Mbizo's master, arched its great length above the mud, then died, falling onto the riverbank with a heavy, wet sound. Only the face remained human, the features twisted into a grimace of unbearable torment.

After that, Mbizo became the servant—and later the student—of the diviner. He was able to work great wonders himself. But neither he nor his fellow villagers ever strayed to the part of the riverbank poisoned by the evil of the *mulombe.*

The Haunted Grove

(Canada)

$\mathbf{A}$ man named Angus lived with his wife, not far from a hill where a grove of maples grew around a single beech tree. The grove wasn't dense—just about half an acre of thinly wooded land. The trees were so far apart that one could easily look between the dark trunks and see the countryside beyond.

One autumn afternoon, Angus climbed this hill on his way home from town. Passing through the grove, he stopped when he heard someone chopping a tree. He was curious, because the grove belonged to a neighbor who had left it untouched for years. As the chopping continued, he looked all around. But he could see no woodsman with an ax.

At last he shouted, "Who's there?"

There was no reply, although anyone close would have heard him. The chopping ceased for a few moments, but as his shout died away, it began again. Puzzled, Angus returned home. But he did not say anything to his wife. By the time he was safely in their kitchen, he had put the event out of his mind.

A few days later he was on the same path when he heard the same *chop, chop, chop*ping. Again he saw no one. But this time he told his wife and friends what had happened. Many of the townspeople went to the grove in groups or alone, but they heard nothing. They searched the little wood, but found no wood chips or cut trunks. There was no mark of any kind anywhere in the grove.

His neighbors made fun of Angus, but his wife felt it was a warning of some kind. She could not guess who was warning Angus or what the warning meant. Still, she cautioned him to stay away from the grove. But Angus was stubborn; he ignored both his neighbors' laughter and his wife's advice, and continued to walk near the wood. When he was alone, he always heard the mysterious ax at work. But when he was with someone else, the ax was silent.

Weeks sped on and brought winter and a heavy snowfall. The snow that drifted over roads and fields did not clog the grove: The trees protected it from the drifts. Now Angus would always use the grove as a shortcut from town to his house. He told his wife with grim humor, "The man in the wood seems pleased I go that way. His chopping is louder and faster than ever." But his wife just begged him again to avoid the grove.

And again Angus ignored her advice. He continued to walk twice a day through the grove. Every day the ax chopped more loudly. But Angus had grown quite used to it.

Late one afternoon his neighbor, the owner of the grove, went with his sons to chop down the lone beech tree among the maples. The tree had died sometime before. It was only fit for firewood now. As they began to chop, one of the sons said, "Wouldn't it be a laugh if we are cutting down the very tree that Angus's ghost has been working on for so long." Soon the tree was swaying and shivering as if it was all but ready to fall.

That evening Angus crossed the grove as usual, hearing the familiar *chop, chop, chop*ping. But it was not the mysterious woodsman this time. It was his neighbor's ax that delivered the solid strokes he heard.

Now, Angus had cut trees all his life and he recognized the sound of the stroke when a tree-cutting task is all but done. But he thought this was only more goblin's trickery, so he paid no attention. He calmly continued on his way.

Suddenly his blood froze as he heard his neighbor's voice cry, "Angus! Look out, man!"

The man's sons caught up the cry. There was noise everywhere—the crashing of branches and the rushing of feet mingled with more warning shouts.

Poor Angus fell with the enormous tree upon him. When at last the burden was removed and his crushed body carried home, there were men who heard inhuman laughter among the trees. They were sure it came from the something that had lured unhappy Angus to his doom.

The Tiger Woman

(*China*)

There was once a young hunter whose father and grandfather before him had also been huntsmen. While they pursued many different creatures, they most prized the hides of tigers from the southern mountains. Over the years, the family had hunted the tigers nearly to extinction.

When the young man, named Ts'ui T'ao, had slain two male tigers—one very old, one quite young—it seemed that he had finished off the last ones. For a long time he searched, finding no trace of any remaining tigers. He was happy to return home with the two pelts; but he was sad to think that the mountains would never again yield up such prizes.

To T'ao's delight, the following year brought reports that another tiger had been spotted in the same mountains. Eagerly he set out for the hunt early one morning.

Toward evening, he reached an inn near a mountain pass. This was a place he had often visited. But to his surprise, the place was deserted. Weeds choked the courtyard; dust filled the rooms. The hour was growing late, however, so the hunter decided to take shelter for the night. He found a room that still had bedding, and a lamp and a candle.

He had just spread out his blankets and was getting

ready for bed when he heard a sound outside. At first he thought it was the wind banging the unlocked gate. Then, in the brilliant moonlight, he saw a huge paw push the gate open. A minute later, he saw a tigress move to the center of the yard. There it sat, its golden eyes staring into the hunter's own.

T'ao had just reached for his bow when the beast suddenly began to shrug off its skin. From beneath the striped pelt there appeared a girl of extraordinary beauty. She was well-dressed and wore jewels of the rarest sort. She bowed toward the window where T'ao stood, his hand halfway to his bow.

After a moment, the young man invited her inside, though he kept an arrow ready. In the hall, the young woman told him her sad tale: "I lived with my father and brother nearby. Somehow they offended one of the mountain spirits. He slew them both, then cast a spell upon me, so that I must prowl the mountains as a tiger by day, though I can put off my skin for an hour each night. The only way I can break the spell is to find someone who will agree to be my husband. Such a man must be brave as well as kind. All others who have heard my story have run away in fear. Will you run away also?"

T'ao gazed at her lovely face, wet with tears, and fell hopelessly in love. "I will gratefully welcome you as my bride."

The young woman rose, smiling now, and picked up the tiger skin. "You have filled my heart with joy," she said. "I will put away my sorrow as easily as I put aside this unhappy reminder of my suffering." Then she took the pelt and hid it, refusing to tell T'ao what she had done with it.

So T'ao, who had hoped to bring home a tiger's hide, brought home a bride instead.

The two were very happy. T'ao's widowed father welcomed his son's wife. By agreement, neither T'ao nor his bride told anyone about the spell that she had been under. In time they had two sons.

T'ao gave up his life of hunting and became a rich and powerful man in his town. Soon he was offered a position at the emperor's court. He decided to move his household to the imperial city. Even his aged father would go.

The journey would take them through the mountain pass and near the deserted inn where they had first met. Though T'ao was anxious to take up his duties at court, he agreed with his wife's request that they stay for a day or two at the abandoned inn. "I want to recall our first meeting," she said, smiling sweetly.

While their servants cleaned the rooms and brewed tea for T'ao's father, husband and wife strolled in the moonlit courtyard. Nearby, their two young sons played tag.

"So many years have passed since I met you," said T'ao laughingly.

"Yet to me it seems like no more than a minute," his wife answered. "This night is the fulfillment of my dearest dreams. Now, come, I have a surprise for you." She took him by the hand and led him to a small outbuilding. Puzzled but agreeable, her husband followed.

From its hiding place beneath a loose board, she removed the tiger skin she had worn. Holding it in her hands, the woman said, "As I told you long ago, my father and young brother were slain nearby. But it was no mountain spirit who slew them. It was a young hunter, Ts'ui T'ao, who killed them and took their skins because they were tigers.

"As I wept for them, I vowed to punish you and your

whole family. So I have bided my time, waiting for the proper moment. Now I will slay your father as you slew mine. Your sons will pay with their lives for the life of my brother. And you will know the bitter taste of loss, even as I taste sweet revenge.''

Instantly she slipped on the tiger skin and became a raging beast that slew T'ao, his aged father, the boys, and everyone else. Then, roaring and bounding, the tigress disappeared into the mountain fastness.

Peacock's Ghost

(United States—Louisiana)

Not long ago, a young man named John Peacock lived in New Orleans. One day he learned that he had inherited a farm from a distant cousin of his. The farm was in the Louisiana backcountry. This came as a surprise, since his cousin had lived all his life in Europe and had never spoken of such a thing. In any case, John was eager to drive up and see what the farm looked like. But the place, called Peacock's Farm, was miles away, where roads were poorly marked, if at all.

John soon became hopelessly lost trying to find the farm. At a crossroads, he saw an old woman, sitting in a rocker on the sagging porch of a crumbling house. Behind the house were the remains of a barn and a shed, choked with brambles and vines. The woman was wearing an old white shift, and her uncombed white hair gave her a wild look.

Since there was no one else around, the young man parked his car and strolled to the porch.

"Can you tell me how to find Peacock's Farm?" he asked.

"I kin tell you," the woman said. "But you don' want ter go thar."

"Why not?" John asked. "The place belongs to me now."

"Mebbe. Mebbe not," she said. "Anyhow, I got a story ter tell you. If you lissen an' you still want ter go thar, I'll show you the way."

John Peacock agreed; then he fanned himself with his hat as she began:

"Years ago, ole man Peacock died an' lef' a heap o' property ter his chillun. An' he give ev'ry one a farm. There was one mo' farm lef' over. 'Twas a good farm an' the house all furnished up, but no one did keer ter live thar, fer they all said the house was haanted.

"One o' the sons—Micah Peacock—said he wan't no way a-feared. Said he could lay that ghost if they'd give him the farm. Th' others tole him the place was his if he could lay the ghost so's ter live thar.

"Well, Micah went at night ter the house, takin' his Bible along. He sat thar a-readin' it backward and forward: He didn' mind it none whether the ghost came a-nigh or not. Sho' nuff, the ghost come along while he was a-readin'. It went all about thro' the house, so's Micah could hear it goin' inter the diffunt rooms an' a-movin' things thisaway an' thataway. But he didn' let on ter hear the ghost—no indeed, he kep' a-readin' away in his Bible.

"After a while the ghost blowed out his lamp, but he jes' lighted it an' read on. Then he went inter the bedroom an' lay down. That sort o' made the ghost mad, so's it come inter the bedroom an' Micah seed it, like as if it was a real person.

"Anyhow, then he seed the ghost reach out an arm, long an' skinny-like, under the bed, an' jes' turn it over with him on it. But he only crep' out from under it an' went back inter the kitchen an' begun ter read away in his Bible. An' thar he stayed all night. Afore day, the ghost come once mo' an' said, 'If you come back yere again, yore a dead man.'

"Well, the nex' night Micah Peacock come back again, yes indeed: an' he'd got two preachers ter come along an' try to lay that ghost. One was a Methodis' an' the other was a Catholic. They both brought their Bibles, an' all of 'em kep' a-readin' forward an' backward. 'Twan't no time at all till that ghost come again, an' then it just went on mos' outrageous.

"The Methodis', he didn' stay ter hear much o' the racket. Out he run an' never come back. The Catholic, he held out a good bit, but afore long *he* run an' lef' Peacock ter stay it out by himself.

"Well, they say the ghost never spoke ter him no mo'; but sho' nuff, in the mornin', thar was Peacock a-lyin' dead with his head cut clean off—yes indeed, sir!—an thar ain' no one ever try ter lay that ghost since."

"Well, I've been warned," said John Peacock impatiently. "Now give me the directions you promised. Let me tell you, any ghost that crosses me will find he's—"

"Who tole you it were a *he*?" the old woman said. She stood up from the rocker and began to grow longer and thinner. Her bony hand locked on to young Peacock's wrist; her grip was as painful as a metal vise. He was afraid she was going to snap his wrist bone like balsa wood.

"Yep," she said, suddenly letting go of him. "You been warned. This yere is Peacock's Farm. Still want ter stay?"

But John was halfway to his car. When he looked back, he saw only the old rocker bobbing on the porch.

John drove as quick as he could back to New Orleans. There he burned the deed to Peacock's Farm. But for the rest of his life, there was a bruise, like the imprint of long, thin fingers, around his wrist.

Israel and the Werewolf

(Poland—Jewish traditional)

Long ago, there was an orphan named Israel, who depended on his own wit and the charity of others to survive. When little more than a child himself, he earned his keep by walking young students of his village to and from the school next to the synagogue, some distance away.

Often, Israel did not lead the children in his care right to school. Sometimes he would take them for walks in the wood to explore the natural world. The boy believed that a person could learn about God from the beauties and secrets of nature, as well as from Holy Scripture. While they wandered, Israel amused the youngsters with riddles and stories; and he taught them simple hymns.

Deep in the forest lived an old woodcutter who was greatly troubled. At heart he was a simple man who wished harm to no one. But he hid himself away in the forest because of his affliction. Every night demons entered his body, turning him into a werewolf. He would drop to all fours, howl like a wolf, and chase rabbits and other small woodland creatures to devour them.

The sound of Israel and the children singing might have eased his sorrow. But the devils who enslaved him were not pleased to hear innocent voices singing hymns of praise to the Lord, for this is the purest prayer of all. And

Israel's holiness was more than the demons could face. They complained to Satan himself; and the King of Evil decided he would confront Israel.

One night after the woodcutter had taken on his werewolf form, Satan entered his body, removed the man's troubled heart, and replaced it with his own. This time when morning came, the woodcutter remained a monster.

When Israel and his young companions entered the wood, planning a breakfast of wild berries, they sensed a change in the forest. No birds sang; no breeze stirred the leaves or pine needles. Then the children discovered a clump of berry bushes and began filling their mouths and pockets, laughing all the while. But Israel remained watchful.

Suddenly the werewolf burst into the clearing. The other children ran screaming in all directions, but Israel bravely stood his ground. Israel recited all the prayers he knew, but they had no effect on the creature that slouched toward him, growing larger and larger with each passing moment. He sang a hymn of praise, but still the huge creature came nearer. Then the werewolf opened its jaws as wide as the gates to Satan's kingdom, and prepared to swallow him.

But Israel simply walked forward, feeling the power of Heaven all around him. He marched straight into the maw of the beast. In its belly, he moved along a dark passageway. He was drawn forward by a sound like a distant drumbeat.

Then Israel entered a great cavern walled in red and white. Above him, hanging from a branch of flesh, was the creature's heart—not the heart of the woodcutter or the heart of a wolf, but the black heart of the King of Evil.

Still moved by the power of Heaven, Israel reached up

and plucked the heart. Cradling it in his hands, he walked out into the night. Hours had passed while he was inside the monster—though it seemed a short time to Israel. When he left the body of the beast, the ground shook under his feet. Then it split open. The heart slipped from his hands and rolled into the fissure. Instantly the earth closed over it.

Israel stood before a corpse. What previously had been a werewolf, fanged and furred and clawed, was now only the body of the gentle old woodcutter. He lay still and smiling, peaceful at last. Israel said a prayer for the man. Then he gathered the children—still frightened and hiding—and led them home. The light of the full moon revealed a safe path before them.

Hoichi the Earless

(*Japan—from Lafcadio Hearn*)

In Japan long ago, near where the sea battle of Dan-no-ura had been fought centuries before, there lived a poor blind man named Hoichi. He was famous for his skill in reciting poetry and for playing upon the *biwa,* a stringed instrument like a lute. A priest of the local temple invited Hoichi to live there. Hoichi accepted, paying for his keep by playing for the priests.

One hot summer night, when the priests were away, Hoichi tried to cool himself by sitting on the porch of his sleeping room. Softly he practiced on his *biwa.* At midnight, he heard steps cross the garden and halt in front of him. A strange commanding voice called, "Hoichi!"

"Hai!" answered the blind man, frightened by the menace in the voice. "I am blind! I cannot know who calls."

"There is nothing to fear," the stranger said, speaking more gently. "I have been sent to you with a message. My lord, a very powerful man, is staying nearby with many of his nobles. He wishes to view the scene of the battle of Dan-no-ura. He has heard of your skill in reciting the story of the battle. He desires to hear you. Come with me to the house, where he is waiting."

Hoichi felt honored to be asked to play for the man's master. He put on his sandals, took his *biwa,* and went with the stranger. The fellow led the musician carefully, but forced him to walk very fast. The hand that guided him was like iron, and the clank of the warrior's stride meant that he was fully armed.

Presently the man halted; Hoichi sensed that they had come to a large gateway. He was puzzled, because he could not remember any such gate in that part of town. But he forgot the thought when the gate was unbarred. "Leave your sandals before we enter," said the soldier.

When Hoichi had done so, they entered a space that echoed like a great hall. Hoichi heard hurrying feet, sliding screens, and chattering women. Then he was led to a platform with silk pillows. A vast number of people had gathered—the rustling of their robes was like that of forest leaves; their voices hummed like swarms of bees. Then all became silent.

"Recite the story of the battle at Dan-no-ura," his guide ordered. So Hoichi recited the chant of the fight on the bitter sea. He made his *biwa* sound like straining oars and rushing ships, like the hiss of arrows, men's shouts, the crash of steel upon helmets, and the death cries and the splashes of the slain falling into the bloody waters.

At the part where every remaining man, woman, and child of the Taira clan perished at the hands of their enemies, his listeners uttered one long anguished cry. Then they wept and wailed so loudly that the blind man was frightened by the violent grief he had loosed. But gradually the wailing and sobbing died away.

In the stillness, Hoichi heard his guide say, "My lord is so impressed with your skill, he desires you to perform before him for the next six nights. After that, he makes his return journey. Tomorrow night I will bring you here. But you must not tell anyone what has happened. My lord is traveling secretly, on a matter of great importance. He commands your silence."

Hoichi said nothing to the priests about his midnight adventure. The next night the soldier came for him, and he gave another performance. But this time, his absence from the temple was noticed. In the morning, his friend the priest said, "We have been anxious about you, Hoichi. Where have you been?"

Hoichi only said, "I had private business to attend to."

The priest suspected something was wrong. He did not ask more questions, but he told his servants to follow Hoichi if he left after dark. When Hoichi departed that evening, the men followed. But they lost him in the darkness and rain of a summer storm. Hoichi, who had gone alone, had walked very fast—most unusual for a blind man on a road that was in need of repair.

As they neared the shore, the servants were startled by the sound of a *biwa,* furiously played in the cemetery of the Taira Clan. In the blackness, ghost fires and will-o'-the-wisps darted here and there. Running to the cemetery, the servants found Hoichi sitting alone and chanting the story of Dan-no-ura. Above the tombs around him, the fires of the dead burned like candles.

"Hoichi!" the servants cried. "You are bewitched."

But the blind man did not seem to hear. He continued to chant until the story was finished. Then the ghost fires went out, and Hoichi awoke as if from a deep sleep.

The next day the priest forced Hoichi to tell all about his midnight adventures. Then the priest said, "Hoichi, your skill has brought you into great danger! You have been spending your nights among the tombs of the Taira clan. By obeying the call of the dead, you have put yourself in their power. When they have finished with you, they will tear you to pieces. But there is a way to save you."

Before sundown, while a naked Hoichi shivered, the priest painted holy signs all over his body—even on the soles of his feet. Then the priest said, "Tonight, seat yourself on the porch and wait. You will be called. Whatever happens, do not answer and do not move. If you stir or call for help, you will be torn apart."

So Hoichi sat as still as the *biwa* not far from him. Soon he heard steps approach and stop directly in front of him.

"Hoichi!" the deep voice called. But the blind man held his breath and sat motionless. The voice called his name again and again, growing angrier each time.

At last the gruff voice muttered, "Here is his *biwa,* but I see nothing of the man who plays it—except his two ears! So that explains why he did not answer: He has no mouth. There is nothing left but his ears. I will take those ears to my lord as proof that I did as much as I could to bring him the musician."

Hoichi felt his ears gripped by fingers of iron and torn off. Great as the pain was, he gave no cry. The heavy footfalls departed and faded away. Still he sat, not daring to move.

When the priest returned, he cried, "Poor Hoichi! In my haste, I forgot to paint holy signs upon your ears. But awful as it is, you will never again be troubled by those ghosts."

———

Hoichi soon recovered from his injuries. The story of his adventure spread far and wide and made him famous. Many noble persons came to hear him perform. They paid him richly, and he became a wealthy man. But he was always known as *Mimi-nashi-Hoichi:* Hoichi the Earless.

A Snap of the Fingers

(Mexico)

Many years ago, Miguel, a boy from the country, visited his grandfather in Mexico City. The old man lived on a pleasant tree-shaded street; but there was one house he shunned. He warned his grandson, "Stay away from that place. The owner, Don Rodrigo, is evil. It is said he serves the devil."

Then Miguel's grandfather explained that Don Rodrigo had been a captain in the Spanish royal army. He had fought so well that the king of Spain had rewarded him by making him a don and giving him official duties in Mexico City.

At first Don Rodrigo had been an honest and respected man of very modest means. Then, one night, a raven had flown to his window during a storm. After this, Don Rodrigo became rich and powerful, but corrupt. He never went to church, and he openly made fun of all things holy. This offended his neighbors. Worse yet, he named the raven El Diablo. And it truly was a devil: Miguel's grandfather assured the boy that no one doubted this for a minute.

Don Rodrigo would sit at a window or on one of the several balconies of his house, snapping his fingers. Then the raven would come and perch beside him.

"I have heard from Don Rodrigo's servants," Miguel's

grandfather said, "that the bird soils the floors and furnishings, tears the chairs and drapes with its beak, and throws down and shatters the glass and china. But when Don Rodrigo storms at his servants about the damage— and he is a most violent man, Miguel, who uses violent language—the servants just tell him the raven made the mischief. Then Don Rodrigo becomes calm again. 'If it is the work of the devil,' he says, 'then it is well done!' Such a wicked man!" Miguel's grandfather said. "You must stay away from him and that accursed bird."

But Miguel was curious. He would often watch Don Rodrigo in the street. The man lived richly, eating from dishes of solid silver carried by servants wearing clothes embroidered with gold. Yet he dressed like a beggar. Over his shirt and breeches he wore a long cape reaching almost to his heels, which the king of Spain had given him. It bore the emblem of the king himself. When Don Rodrigo wore it, he commanded respect. Yet even this cape, Miguel saw, was shabby and greasy and covered with stains.

The raven, El Diablo, was always preening itself. Its feathers were glossy and unruffled. Secretly Miguel put out corn and bread, and the bird often came to him. It would gobble up the food greedily, then watch him. From the way it looked at him—head cocked to one side, eyes staring into his own—Miguel almost felt it was going to speak to him. Then from the nearby house would come the snapping of Don Rodrigo's fingers and the call "El Diablo!" and the bird would fly off.

Two days before Miguel was to return home, Don Rodrigo discovered him feeding the raven in the alley beside his grandfather's house. "Traitor!" the man shrieked at the bird, and he tried to grab it. But the raven gave a mocking cry and flew to safety. Then the man turned on

Miguel. "Has the miserable creature struck a bargain with you? *Tell me!*" he yelled.

Confused and frightened, Miguel fled down the alley while Don Rodrigo shouted threats after him. The boy did not tell his grandfather what had happened. But he swept every trace of corn and bread crumbs from his windowsill. Then he fastened his shutters.

That night, as he lay in bed, Miguel heard wings beating outside the shutters. Claws slashed at the wood; he heard the *tunk-tunk-tunk* of the raven's razor-sharp beak as it tried to break in. In a panic, Miguel took his crucifix off the wall and laid it against the shutters. Instantly the attack stopped. Then the boy heard the faint, impatient snapping of Don Rodrigo's fingers. Then nothing.

The next morning his grandfather's house was abuzz with amazing news. During the night Don Rodrigo's servants had been awakened by terrifying shrieks and pounding from the master's bedroom. When they finally broke down the heavy doors, they found the signs of a terrible struggle: Bedclothes were tossed about, chairs overturned, the doors of the wardrobe were nearly torn off, and most of the clothing inside had been thrown onto the floor. Blood was splashed about, and bloody raven feathers lay in every corner. But there was no other trace of Don Rodrigo or El Diablo.

"Their master, the devil, has carried them off," Miguel's grandfather said. "That is a fitting end to both."

On his last night, Miguel slept with his shutters fastened and the cross in place. Once, he thought he heard the whirr of wings outside, but he couldn't be sure.

For many reasons, Miguel did not return to Mexico City to visit his grandfather for several years. When he did, he found the house of Don Rodrigo empty and falling to ruin. People would cross themselves and hurry past the place.

It was said that the house was haunted. On certain nights, Miguel was told, the ghostly figure of Don Rodrigo could be seen and heard, snapping his fingers and calling, "El Diablo!" Then, with an answering caw, the raven would fly out of the darkness and settle on a windowsill of the dark house, and Don Rodrigo would stroke the bird's back. Then both would vanish.

On Miguel's first night at his grandfather's house, there was a tremendous storm. The lightning and thunder kept him awake. Between thunderclaps, Miguel thought he heard a sound like fingers snapping. Opening his window, he became sure that the sound came from Don Rodrigo's house.

As he listened, the sound seemed to hypnotize him. He felt he had to obey the summons the way the raven had done. He quickly dressed himself, took a lantern, and followed the sound to Don Rodrigo's house.

The force of the storm had blown the front door open. Like a dreamer, Miguel crossed dusty rooms and climbed the staircase to the second floor. Lightning revealed the open door of a large chamber at the end of the hall. Past a bed, the double doors of a huge wardrobe gaped on the very heart of darkness.

From inside came the snapping, louder than ever. Miguel climbed inside the wardrobe. Something urged him to run his hand over the wooden wall at the back. He discovered a peg that moved, opening the hidden door to a secret room.

In the lamplight, Miguel saw the mummified remains of Don Rodrigo; the dust-dry figure was wrapped in the dirty

old cape with the king's emblem. But it was spattered with dark blotches. And there were marks upon the face, and wounds still visible on the mummy's chest, that Miguel guessed had been made by the beak and claws of a raven.

Then, to his horror, the right hand snapped its fingers. Half expecting the remains to sit up and speak, Miguel backed away. The next instant the raven flew in and landed on the mummy's wrist. It cocked its head and studied Miguel with glowing eyes.

Too frightened to speak, Miguel just shook his head. The bird's eyes burned into his own. Again he shook his head. With a dart of its beak, the raven snapped off the mummy's thumb and middle finger. Then it flew to Miguel's shoulder, and dropped the finger bones into the boy's shirt.

The bones sliding down between his shirtfront and bare chest, and the weight of the bird on his shoulder, shocked Miguel into action. He swung his lantern around, and the raven hopped back to the mummy with a cry. Miguel, mad with fear for his very soul, threw the lantern at the bird. It flew screeching into the corner as the cape caught fire, and the mummy was wrapped in flames.

The raven cried again. Miguel pressed his hands to his ears and fled through the darkened house. The flames followed, setting the place ablaze. Outside, he felt a sudden pinching of the flesh at his stomach—as though some tiny animal were biting him. Horrified, he remembered the finger bones still in his shirt. In disgust, he clawed them free and hurled them into one of the urns beside his grandfather's door. He sealed his shutters with a cross, then prayed until he fell into an exhausted sleep.

The next day he was told that lightning had struck Don Rodrigo's house and burned it to the ground. Miguel tried to convince himself that he had had a dream. But the finger bones at the bottom of the urn told him the truth of what had happened. He buried them in the farthest corner of the garden.

Never again did the ghostly fingers of Don Rodrigo summon the raven. But no matter where he went, Miguel could not put aside the horrors of that night. Worse was the belief that he had only to snap his own fingers and whisper "El Diablo!" and the bird would come to him. When his life grew difficult, he found it hard to resist the temptation for wealth and power that was only a snap of the fingers away. And this struggle was the worst torture of all.

Narrow Escape

(United States—California)

Tessa waved goodbye to her friend Joanie as she started the engine of her car. Then she groaned as the gas gauge flickered above Empty. She had been so upset and angry with her father, she had forgotten to fill the gas tank. One more disaster in an already disastrous night. First the blowup with her father, who had forbidden her to drive alone after dark. Then her own storming out into the night, determined to see her friends. She could just imagine the scene that was coming when she got back home.

She knew her father thought he was acting for her own good. Somewhere out there was the murderer the media called the Gold Country Killer. His victims were scattered across the part of northern California where gold had first been discovered. He attacked only people who were alone: a hiker, a fisherman, someone whose car had stalled out on a lonely stretch of road.

Tessa's anger came flooding back. It was her father's fault they had moved from San Francisco to Parkhurst, which was about as middle-of-nowhere as it got. He was a writer: He loved being away from the people and noise and movement that Tessa missed. She had argued against the move, but her parents had overruled her. The family didn't even live in town, but way beyond. Going to school, visiting friends, everything was a hassle. And now her father wanted to ground her after dark.

To make things worse, the evening had fizzled. Brad Sanders and the other guys from the football team had decided to bag dinner at Joanie's. So it had been girls' night: porking out on pizzas (with more than half of them still in their greasy boxes—thanks, guys!) and watching the *Scream* flicks on video (not real thrilling—Tessa and her friends had seen them too many times already).

Tessa looked at her watch: 10:35 P.M. The only gas station was the Fast-Fill on the other side of Parkhurst. She made a right and headed for it, hoping that creepy Dale Robbins wouldn't be working as cashier. He was always trying to make a date with her. It had gotten to the point where she avoided him every chance she could.

Her luck was also running on empty: She recognized Dale's rusty old red pickup truck even before she saw the tall, skinny boy inside the glass booth. Dale was wearing a stupid baseball cap with the Fast-Fill logo; it made him look even geekier. She parked at the pump farthest from the booth. Dale waved to her. Geez! she thought, how bad is this night gonna get?

When she pushed her money through the slot, Dale said, "It's nice to see you, Tessa."

"I want ten dollars of unleaded," she said, hoping to cut off the small talk before it began.

"I'd really like to ask you something," he said.

"Some other time," she said. "I'm late, and my father is gunning for me." She walked back to her car, waiting in a pool of light beside a shadowy clump of trees. She heard the click as Dale turned on the pump. When she had gassed up, Tessa decided to make a quick stop at the rest room. Her bladder was running on full.

She circled the cashier's booth, thankful that Dale was taking care of another customer. When she left the rest room, the other car was gone. But Dale had suddenly gone bananas, waving and pointing and yelling her name through the loudspeaker of the booth.

Tessa hurried back to her car, yanking the unlocked door open so that she could make a fast getaway.

The speaker over the gas pump crackled. "Tessa, you've got to get out of the car, now!" Dale yelled.

"Get a life!" she shouted. She slammed the door and burned an impressive amount of rubber as she left the Fast-Fill.

But when she turned onto the main road, her rearview mirror showed a set of headlights pulling out of the Fast-Fill. She guessed the other customer had been using the men's room while she had been next door. She drove slowly, dreading the angry showdown waiting for her at home.

A short way up the main road, she turned onto the little-used side road that led home. Glancing in her mirror, she saw that the other car had turned in after her. She could see only its headlights in the darkness. Strange! Her family had very few neighbors, and they usually weren't out this late.

Suddenly the headlights of the car following her came on to full beam. Not knowing what was up, but afraid this was a deliberate attempt to blind her, perhaps run her off the road, Tessa accelerated. But as fast as she accelerated, so did the car behind. She could not get away from the glaring lights that flooded the inside of her car,

though she tilted the mirror down to keep from being blinded.

Still hoping it was one of her neighbors who had partied too heartily and couldn't tell his high beams from a hole in the ground, Tessa turned off the road onto the narrow lane that wound up through the trees to her house. There were no other homes along the lane.

"Good riddance, creep!" she muttered.

To her horror, the car behind followed, its headlights blazing. By this time she was convinced she was being stalked. In panic she put maximum pedal to the metal. Her car lurched ahead. Taking the curves at speeds she had never attempted before, she prayed she would reach her parents' house before it was too late.

The car behind followed relentlessly.

Rounding a curve and checking her rearview mirror, Tessa caught a glimpse of her pursuer through a break in the trees. It was Dale's rusty red pickup! She grew even more terrified. Was Dale the Gold Country Killer? She thought of all the *Scream* twists she had watched on video earlier. Why not? Who'd suspect the school fool of murder? Or was he simply angry that she had blown him off at the Fast-Fill? In either case, it wouldn't be pretty if he caught her.

She managed to get a little extra *oomph* out of her car. I'm going to make it, she told herself. She knew her father would be watching for her. The ex-Marine would make short work of a wuss like Dale.

Then she hit a pothole. The car fishtailed. She tried to remember all the rules about steering into the swerve and keeping control. Nothing worked. Her hands gripping the wheel, she slid across the oncoming lane and into a drainage ditch.

Stunned for a moment, Tessa struggled with her seat belt. The rusty red pickup squealed to a halt on the shoulder across from her. Dale leapt out, carrying a tire jack.

"Oh, no," she whispered, still struggling with the straps. She released the belt just as Dale jerked open the door. "Don't hurt me!" Tessa screamed, but Dale just threw her out of the car. She fell to the gravel, cutting her hands and knees. Like a frightened crab, she tried to scuttle away from him.

But Dale ignored her. He yanked open the passenger door behind the driver's seat. A dark figure sprang out, knocking Dale into the roadway, sending the tire iron spinning toward her. The man had his hands around Dale's throat. Tessa saw a length of knotted cord; the guy was trying to strangle Dale.

In an instant, Tessa realized that Dale had risked his life to rescue her.

She picked up the tire iron, swung it over her head as hard as she could, and knocked Dale's attacker unconscious.

Tessa knelt beside Dale. "You saved my life," she said.

"Ditto," he said, rubbing his throat. He picked up his Fast-Fill cap from the road and dusted it against his jeans. Then he replaced it. "I saw someone crawl into the back of your car just as you were leaving. I tried to warn you, but—"

"But I blew it," said Tessa. "Maybe I've blown a few things this evening."

"Anyhow, I followed with my headlights on to keep that guy ducking down in the backseat."

"You're a hero," she said.

"Hey, no big deal," he said. "But we better hurry and

call the cops. I'm gonna follow you home, as soon as we get your car out of the ditch."

"I just realized something," Tessa said. She knocked his cap off his head, then tousled his hair. "Lose the cap. Work with the hair. There's hope for you yet." And she grinned at him.

The Black Fox

(United States—Connecticut)

Not long after the Revolutionary War, a hunter named James Winslow, who lived near the Salmon River, took his rifle down from the wall and stepped out of his cabin. His dog followed. In the cold, bright night, his friend, Occom, a Mohegan, waited. The Indian was wrapped in a deerhide cape against the biting wind. Around them, the moonlight lay bright on the deep snowdrifts.

The two men greeted each other briefly, then set out into the pine forest. As they followed the dog, the only sound was the faint crunch of their feet on the crusted snow. They were hunting a fox that had troubled the countryside for weeks. It slipped into barns and smokehouses and henhouses, and boldly made off with piglets and cured meats and chickens. Those who had caught sight of the creature escaping with a fat hen clamped in its jaws swore that it was coal black. "It was like a shadow running across the snow," one man said.

The local farmers had offered a large reward for the fox's hide. This was what drew James Winslow and Occom into the freezing winter night.

The dog bounded on ahead, searching for a trace of the fox. Keeping his voice low, Occom said, "The *moigu*—the shaman—did not want me to hunt with you tonight. He said the fox we seek is a thing that is evil. No bullet or arrow can slay it.''

"Do you believe that?" Winslow challenged. "I've seen enough half-chewed hams and bloody chicken feathers to know that this fox fills his belly like any other fox.''

Occom shrugged. "The *moigu* is an old man. His ways are the old ways. I am a Christian now. I think like the white man." He smiled grimly. "I think the fox will give up his hide to us tonight. And the farmers will give up their gold to us soon after this.''

Suddenly the dog froze, growled, then pointed with his uplifted paw. Winslow cocked his rifle; Occom bent his bow. The jet-black fox watched them from the top of a snow-covered boulder. It almost seemed to be daring them to take action.

Winslow fired. Occom loosed his arrow. The creature should have been dead twice over. But somehow bullet and arrow missed. The creature gave a yip almost like a laugh, and scurried off.

The dog charged after it. The men followed. From time to time, the puzzled dog seemed to lose the scent. Then he would pick it up again, and the chase would continue. The hunters followed deeper and deeper into the woods.

Then the dog halted at the edge of a clearing. Across a patch of moonlit snow was the fox's den, a hollow at the base of an outcropping of rock. The two hunters saw a flicker of black tail as the fox disappeared inside.

The dog was strangely silent. When Winslow snapped his fingers and tried to urge the dog forward, the poor creature simply whined. It would not budge. "Fool animal!'' Winslow snarled. He signaled Occom, and the two moved toward the shadowed mouth of the fox's lair.

"We've got him trapped," said Winslow, raising his rifle.

Occom nodded as he fitted an arrow to his bowstring.

From the den came a single yelp.

Behind them, the dog fled howling into the woods.

Then the shadow at the foot of the moonlit rocks began to grow. To the startled men, it seemed as though the shadow had turned to smoke, which was now billowing out at them. In an instant, the dark cloud had swallowed them. Winslow fired his rifle, but the sound was faint, as though buried under layers of cloth, or coming from a great distance.

And then the smothering darkness was gone. The two men stood on the smooth snow that was shining in the moon's rays. There was no trace of rocks or the fox's den. The dog had vanished. At the far side of the open space, the shadow fox appeared. It yipped once, and the chase was on.

The two men ran forward. Nothing existed for them except the hunt. On and on they ran, beneath a moon that never set, in a silent wood where no wind blew, through a night that would never meet day. In the stillness, there was only the movement of the hunters, running and running as the fox scampered on and on, forever ahead of them.

Frightened and hungry, the dog returned to Winslow's cabin. He lay down on the cold stoop.

In the spring, a woodsman found the dog's bones beside the closed door of the deserted cabin. No trace was found of James Winslow or his friend, Occom. But from time to time, a lone hunter will spot two shadowy figures running through the pines. They never answer if called to. They hurry on and are soon lost to sight. The men chase a small shadow that always keeps just ahead—the black fox of Salmon River.

The Mother and Death

(Denmark—from Hans Christian Andersen)

A sorrowful young mother sat beside her sick child, fearing that the little girl would die. Then there was a knock at the door, and an old man came in, wrapped in a great cape, for it was winter. Outside, everything was covered with snow and ice, and the wind blew sharply enough to cut one's face.

The old man trembled with cold. Since the child was quiet for a moment, the mother put on a pot of tea to warm her visitor. The old man sat down and rocked the cradle, and the mother seated herself near him. She seized her sick child's little hand.

"The good God will not take her, will he?" she asked.

The old man—he was Death—nodded in a strange way that might have meant yes or no. Then the mother became so weary that she could not keep her eyes open. She dozed a moment. When she awoke, the old man was gone; and he had taken her child with him.

The poor woman rushed out of the house, crying for her child. Out in the snow, she met an old woman in long black robes. "I saw Death with your child," the old woman said. "He never brings back what he has taken away."

"Tell me which way he went!" cried the mother.

"Before I tell you," said the old woman, "you must sing

me all the songs you have sung to your child. I am Night, and I heard you sing them. I love those songs.''

"I will sing them all for you later," said the mother. "Help me follow my child now."

But Night kept silent. So the mother sang and wept. When she was done, Night said, "Go to the right, into the dark fir wood. Death took that path with your child."

The mother hurried along the path into the wood. Soon she came to a crossroads, and did not know which way to go. She asked a blackthorn bush with icicles hanging from its bare twigs, "Have you see Death go by, with my little child?"

"Yes," replied the bush, "but I will not tell you which way unless you warm me."

The woman threw her cloak over the bush and hugged it, so that the thorns scratched her skin. And the blackthorn put out fresh green leaves and blossomed; then it told her the way she should go.

The mother hurried on, though her skin was bleeding and her limbs ached with weariness. At last she came to a great lake, but it was not frozen enough to hold her. She begged the water, "Carry me across."

"I'm fond of collecting pearls," the lake answered. "Your eyes are two of the clearest I have seen. Weep them into me, and I will carry you over to the great greenhouse where Death grows flowers and trees. Each of these is a human life."

So the mother wept, and her eyes fell into the lake and became two wondrous pearls. Then the lake lifted her up on a wave, and carried her to the opposite shore. There a wonderful house stood, miles in length, all made of glass. But the woman could not see it, since she had lost her eyes.

She called out, "Where will I find Death?"

"He is not here," said a gray-haired woman who tended Death's greenhouse.

"I have come for my child," the blind woman said. "Can you help me?"

The old woman said, "Every human being has a tree or flower of life here. They look like other plants, but their hearts beat. If you give me your long black hair, I will tell you what to do to save your child."

"I will give you that gladly," said the young mother. So she gave away her beautiful hair, and took the old woman's gray hair in exchange.

Then they went into the greenhouse, where flowers and trees of every sort grew. Each had a name; each was a human life. Each belonged to a person who was still alive somewhere in the world.

"Wait here," said the old woman. "When Death comes, don't let him pull up any plant until he returns your child to you. Tell him you will uproot every plant within your reach. That will frighten him, because he has to account for them all. None may be pulled up until he receives word from Heaven."

Suddenly an icy wind rushed through the greenhouse, and the blind mother knew Death had arrived.

"Why are you here?" asked the old man who was Death.

"I have come for my child," the mother answered.

"I only take what God commands," said Death. "I am His gardener. When He commands, I take His trees and flowers and transplant them into the great gardens of Paradise, the unknown land."

Then the woman grasped two little flowers with her two hands. "If you don't give me back my child, I will tear up all your flowers because I am so unhappy."

"And you want to make another mother just as un-happy?"

"Another mother?" said the poor woman, letting go of the flowers.

"Here are your eyes," said Death. "I fished them out of the lake because they gleamed so brightly. Take them, then look down the deep well over here. You will see the future lives of those two flowers you were about to destroy. And you will understand the consequences of tampering with Heaven's commands."

The mother looked down the well and saw the first child, a boy, growing to become a blessing to the world. He brought joy and gladness to everyone around him. It filled her heart with happiness to see this.

Then the mother saw a second child, a girl, growing into a life of care and poverty, misery and woe. And she screamed aloud for terror, because the child was her own.

"Oh, my poor child!" she cried. "Is this what she would suffer if I try to undo what God has willed?"

Death nodded.

Her voice barely a whisper, the mother said, "I was wrong to deny Heaven's will, which is always for the best. Carry her into God's Kingdom, as He has commanded."

Then Death picked the pale flower that was her child's life, and went away with it into the unknown land.

Notes on Sources

CROOKER WAITS. This retelling is based on an account in Katharine M. Briggs, *A Dictionary of British Folk-Tales in the English Language: Part A—Folk Narratives* (New York and London: Routledge & Kegan Paul, 1970; paperback reprint, 1991). Presumably, the three women are fairies, for they wear green, the traditional color of fairy folk. The traveler's kindness in freeing various creatures of the wild has earned him the goodwill of these nature spirits. St. John's Wort is called this because it was gathered on St. John's Eve to ward off evil spirits. The yew tree was thought to have sacred and magical properties. A full discussion can be found in *The Yew Tree: A Thousand Whispers: Biography of a Species,* by Hal Hartzell, Jr. (Eugene, Oregon: Hulogosi Press, 1991). Katharine Briggs notes, "Traditions of malignant and benevolent trees are widespread in England"—probably harking back to pre-Christian nature worship.

YARA-MA-YHA-WHO. This story is retold from accounts in *Myths & Legends of the Australian Aboriginals,* by William Ramsay Smith (London: George G. Harrap, 1930; reprinted as *Aborigine Myths & Legends* (London: Senate/Random House UK, Ltd., 1996), and in *Aboriginal Myths, Legends & Fables,* by A. W. Reed (Chatswood, New South Wales: Reed/William Heinemann Australia, 1982). The Yara-ma-yha-who is a kind of "nursery boogey"—a monster in a cautionary story told to make disobedient children behave or to warn them away from dangers.

THE FATA. I have expanded this story from a very brief narrative (almost an anecdote) and additional information about the *fata* (plural form: *fate*) in *A Field Guide to the Little People,* by Nancy Arrowsmith with George Moorse (New York: Farrar, Straus & Giroux, 1977; paperback reprint, New York: Simon & Schuster, 1978). The *fata* is akin to a fairy or nature spirit. Fata Alcina, mentioned in the story, is the sister of the dreaded Fata Morgana, or Morgan le Fay, who often deceived humans with her powers of enchantment.

THE FIDDLER. Retold and expanded from a brief account in *The Welsh Fairy Books,* by W. Jenkyn Thomas (London: T. Fisher Unwin, 1907; reprint, Cardiff: University of Wales, 1952). Tales of fiddlers who acquire their instruments or arts from the devil, or who challenge the devil to fiddling contests, are well known throughout Europe and America. While the original story does not spell out the exact nature of the "invisible agency" that pulls the fiddler to his fate, it would be safe to assume that the cave is a key to the underworld—either of mischievous fairies or devils—an encounter with either group often proving fatal. Will-o'-the-wisps are phosphorescent lights seen in swamps or other deserted places. Long a puzzle to scientists, they have been explained in a variety of ways in world folklore—as everything from lights carried by elves to the souls of the departed. They are much like the *oni-bi,* or demon fires, mentioned in the note to "Hoichi the Earless."

LAND-OTTER. Adapted from "The Return of Land-Otter" by Mrs. Andrew Lang. Published about 1900, this has been reprinted in *Ghosts and Spirits of Many Lands,* edited by Freya Littledale (Garden City, New York: Doubleday & Company, Inc., 1970). The Tlingit believed that human beings, after death, were born again as babies—part of the great cycle of life. "Supernatural beings were everywhere in the world of the Tlingits,

taking on many different forms. . . . There was the Land Otter
Man, a fierce looking creature who stole people away, deprived
them of their senses, and turned them into land otter men who
tormented humans. Raven, the Trickster, was a major supernatural being." —*America's Fascinating Indian Heritage: The First
Americans—Their Customs, Art, History, and How They Lived,* by
the Editors of *Reader's Digest* (Pleasantville, New York: The
Reader's Digest Association, Inc., 1978). While the Land-Otter
of this tale may have come back to some kind of life through
the power of the supernatural Land Otter Man, his purpose is
benevolent—though, in the end, the parents lose their son a
second time. For a more detailed discussion of the *kushtaka*
(Tlingit for Land Otter Man), consult *Shamans and Kushtakas:
North Coast Tales of the Supernatural,* by Mary Giraudo Beck (Seat-
tle: Alaska Northwest Books, 1991).

A FISH STORY. Retold from a tale published by Mrs. A.M.H.
Christensen in a collection of African American folktales in
1893. A reprint of the original tale can be found under the title
"A Fish Story from Farmville, Virginia," in *American Negro Folklore: Tales, Songs, Memoirs, Superstitions, Proverbs, Rhymes, Riddles,
Names,* by J. Mason Brewer (New York: Quadrangle/New York
Times Book Co., 1968). This cautionary tale about the consequences of eating forbidden fruit is somewhat like the popular
folktale "Tailypo," which I have retold in *Short & Shivery: Thirty
Chilling Tales* (New York: Doubleday, 1987), the first volume of
this series.

APPARITIONS. This is a shortened version of an account that
appeared in *Apparitions: A Narrative of Facts,* by the Rev.
Bourchier Wrey Saville, in 1880. The original chapter has been
reprinted in *The Eerie Book: Tales of the Macabre and Supernatural,*
edited by Margaret Armour (Secaucus, New Jersey: Castle
Books/Book Sales, Inc., 1981). Prussia, part of present-day Ger-

many, was an independent kingdom during the time of this story. The Seven Years' War (1756–1763) was fought between Prussia and other European powers.

THE BIJLI. Adapted from a longer account, titled "The Bijli of the Flaming Torch," by H. Mayne Young, in *Occult Review* 4 (1906). The article was reprinted in *Supernatural Tales from Around the World,* edited by Terri Hardin (New York: Barnes & Noble Books, 1995). A *fakir* (or *fakeer*) is a Hindu wandering holy man who lives by begging, and who often performs feats of magic or endurance (such as remaining perfectly still for long periods of meditation). Hinduism, one of the main religions of India, has a complex mythology, which includes belief in ghosts. The *bijli* of the story seems to be a particular kind of *preta*, or ghost, which is doomed to wander the earth as a kind of punishment for sins committed during life, or because a person did not receive a proper burial. Some merely haunt a place; others can become dangerous to the living. There is also a kind of malignant spirit, or goblin, called a *bhuta*. It is sometimes identified with the *preta*, or ghost, of someone who has met with a violent death. The *bhutas* haunt forests or deserted houses, and always hover above the ground. In modern India, *bhutas* represent the spirits of the dead, whether evil or benevolent.

THE LUTIN. Composed from a number of sources; among the most helpful were *Canadian Folklore: Perspectives on Canadian Culture,* by Edith Fowke (Don Mills, Ontario: Oxford University Press, 1989), and *Were-Wolves and Will-o'-the-wisps: French Tales of Mackinac Retold,* by Dirk Gringhuis (Mackinac Island, Michigan: Mackinac Island State Park Commission, 1974). The creatures are familiar figures in France and parts of Switzerland. They reportedly can appear in any shape, from a small boy to a giant spider, from a traveling flame to a gust of wind. Malicious or playful, they use violence only when humans disturb them or spy on them.

THE HUNDREDTH SKULL. Retold from the original narrative of the same title found in *Myths and Legends of Our Own Land,* by Charles M. Skinner (Philadelphia: J. B. Lippincott Company, 1896, 1924). The story is retold in *Michigan Haunts and Hauntings,* by Marion Kucko (Lansing, Michigan: Thunder Bay Press, 1992). This author sets the story in Michigan, and suggests that the ghosts of the father and grandfather were the agents of Tom Quick's decapitation.

THE OGRE'S ARM. This story is a composite of two tales, "The Goblin of Adachigahara" and "The Ogre of Rashomon," from *The Japanese Fairy Book,* compiled by Yei Theodora Ozaki (London: Archibald Constable & Co., Ltd., 1903; reprint, New York: Dover Publications, Inc., 1967). The two stories blend well— largely because of similar elements, especially the device in both of a hideous, man-eating monster in the guise of a harmless-seeming old woman. I changed the first old woman to a young man to maintain a final element of surprise.

THE HAIRY HANDS. This retelling is based on a variety of accounts, including those in *Witchcraft and Folklore of Dartmoor,* by Ruth E. St. Leger-Gordon (New York: Bell Publishing Company/Crown Books, 1965); *Aidan Chambers' Book of Ghosts and Hauntings,* by Aidan Chambers (Harmondsworth, Middlesex, England: Kestrel Books/Penguin Books Ltd., 1973); and *Myths, Gods and Fantasy: A Sourcebook,* by Pamela Allardice (Bridport, Dorset, England: Prism Press, 1990). Ruth E. St. Leger-Gordon calls the story "yet another example of folklore in the making. As far as I have been able to ascertain, there is no mention or hint of the Hairy Hands before the second decade of the present [twentieth] century."

THE SNOW HUSBAND. This is adapted from the story "The Snow-Man Husband" in *North American Indians,* by Lewis Spence (London: George G. Harrap & Co., Ltd., 1916; reprint,

London: Bracken Books, 1985). Alan Garner has adapted the tale in the form of a prose poem, "Moowis," in *A Book of Goblins* (London: Hamish Hamilton Ltd., 1969; reprint, Harmondsworth, Middlesex, England: Puffin Books/Penguin Books Ltd., 1972). The Algonquin people lived in what is now Canada, in the territory between and north of Lake Ontario and Lake Huron.

THE ZIMWI. Adapted from two interlocked accounts, "A Swahili Tale" and "The Baleful Pumpkin," in *Africa—Myths & Legends,* by Alice Werner (London: George G. Harrap & Co., Ltd., 1933; reprint, London: Studio Editions Ltd., 1995). I have changed some details of the story, and have made the young woman, Mbodze, the heroine who destroys the pumpkin. Many African folktales concern a huge pumpkin, elephant, or other type of swallowing monster. Since it is often an old woman who rescues her village, or a young mother who rescues her children, by letting herself be swallowed up, then cutting everyone free as she destroys the monster, it seemed consistent to keep the young woman as rescuer. For another example, see "Mahada and the Bull Elephant" in *Some Gold and a Little Ivory: Country Tales from Ghana and the Ivory Coast,* edited by Edythe Rance Haskett (New York: John Day Company, 1971). I included an African American variant from Missouri, "Old Sally Cato," in my *Cut From the Same Cloth: American Women of Myth, Legend, and Tall Tale* (New York: Philomel Books, 1993). For a variant with a boy, rather than a girl, as the demon's captive, see "The Pumpkin Spirit," in *Myths and Legends of the Swahili,* by Jan Knappert (London: Heinemann Educational Books, 1970).

WITCHBIRDS. I have shortened and adapted this story from the chapter "Bird Women" in *Human Animals: Werewolves & Other Transformations* by Frank Hamel (London: William Rider & Son, Ltd., 1915; reprint, Hyde Park, New York: University Books,

1969). I have made the nameless young man who falls in love with the youngest witch the boy Léonce for the purposes of dramatic effect and narrative length. The complete original text is reprinted in *Supernatural Tales from Around the World* (op. cit.). "[In] medieval folklore the owl signified night and all that was dark and ugly . . . Jewish folklore believed that Lilith . . . flew about as a night owl, making off with children . . ."— Anthony S. Mercatante in *Zoo of the Gods: Animals in Myth, Legend, & Fable* (New York: Harper & Row, 1974). In West Africa, the owl is considered a witch's sacred bird. The use of magic ointments appears in many European and American tales of witches who are able to fly.

DANGEROUS HILL. Adapted from an account in *True Ghost Stories,* by Marchioness Townshend and Maude Ffoulkes (London: Hutchinson & Company, 1936; reprint, London: Senate/Studio Editions Ltd., 1994). The authors assert that these accounts are "authentic psychic manifestations," and claim that the house and hill described do actually exist. A passing bell is also called a death bell. It is tolled to announce a death.

THE WITCH'S HEAD. Adapted from "Mythology of the Aztecs of Salvador," by C. V. Hartman, in *Journal of American Folk-Lore* 20 (1907); reprinted in *Supernatural Tales from Around the World* (op. cit.). This tale has echoes in Asian tales of ghastly flying heads that detach themselves from their bodies before they go to work their evil. I have retold two of these—"The Berbalangs" from the Philippines and "Rokuro-Kubi" from Japan—in my earlier volume, *Even More Short & Shivery: Thirty Spine-tingling Tales* (New York: Delacorte Press, 1997).

DINKINS IS DEAD. Adapted from the tale "The Man Who Wouldn't Believe He Was Dead" in *The Doctor to the Dead: Grotesque Legends & Folk Tales of Old Charleston,* by John Bennett

(New York: Rinehart & Company, Inc., 1943). Folklorist Maria Leach tells a much-abbreviated version of this story, "Tain't So," in her wonderful collection (perfect for storytelling) *Whistle in the Graveyard: Folktales to Chill Your Bones* (New York: Viking Press, Inc., 1974).

OLD NAN'S GHOST. Adapted from two accounts: "Old Nanny's Ghost" in *A Dictionary of British Folk-Tales in the English Language: Part B—Folk Legends,* by Katharine M. Briggs (New York and London: Routledge & Kegan Paul, 1970; paperback reprint, 1991), and "Old Nan's Ghost" in *Fire Burn: Tales of Witchery,* by Kenneth Radford (New York: Peter Bedrick, 1990). This story touches on two universal themes in ghostlore: the ghost that cannot rest in its grave because of concern about earthly possessions, and the unquiet spirit that seeks repayment of stolen money.

THE INTERRUPTED WEDDING. This retelling blends elements from three parallel accounts: one untitled narrative in *A Field Guide to the Little People* by Nancy Arrowsmith (op. cit.), and two legends, "The Interrupted *Huldre* Wedding at Melbustad" and "The Interrupted *Huldre* Wedding at Norstuhov," both found in *Folktales of Norway,* edited by Reidar Thorwald Christiansen (Chicago: University of Chicago, 1964). *Huldre* is the name given to the elves or fairies that live in hills or mounds. Known throughout Scandinavia, they are called *maanvaki* in Finland, *pysslinger*-folk in Sweden, and by other local names as well. Tall and thin (like the fairies of the British Isles), they are creatures of the night. Between twilight and dawn they tend their cattle, fashion weapons and jewelry and other items, or dance—their favorite occupation. The use of silver bullets to break an evil spell is a familiar motif in world folk literature. Stories of *huldre* folk are still told in the Midwest, where Scandinavian Americans keep alive this storytelling tradition.

THE MULOMBE. This story is fleshed out from an article titled "'Mulombe': A Kaonde Superstition," by "Africanus" in *Journal of the African Society* 20 (1920–21). I created the character of Mbizo to provide a focus and dramatic tension to an account of the creation of a *mulombe* and the demise of the creature and its owner. "Africanus" notes that the account comes from "the Bakaonde, located in the northwest corner of Northern Rhodesia"—now Zimbabwe—"a tribe of the Luba family." He adds, "The *mulombe* is also known as *mulolo*. . . . It is a snake with a man's head, made by certain wizards, that kills the people indicated to it by its owner. . . . The *mulombe* says to his owner, 'I want a person to eat.' The owner then has to indicate a person who it may kill. . . . It is not long, however, before the *mulombe* gets hungry again—hungry for killing, that is, for it does not really eat the victim; in fact it leaves no mark, but the expression 'eat' is used. . . . The owner, if he refuses to indicate a person, becomes ill and will not be cured until he gives way to the importunities of his *mulombe*."

THE HAUNTED GROVE. This widely anthologized bit of Canadian ghostlore was first published in the article "Scottish Myths from Ontario," in *Journal of American Folk-Lore* 6 (1893). No effort is made to explain the nature of the wood spirit or why such a being would haunt Angus. It may be akin to the malicious tree spirit in "Crooker Waits."

THE TIGER WOMAN. Retold from the story "Tiger-Woman," first printed in *Religious Systems of China,* by Jan J. de Groot (Leiden, Netherlands: E. J. Brill, 1907) and reprinted in *Supernatural Tales from Around the World* (op. cit.). De Groot comments, "The most horrid specimens of the tiger-demon class which Chinese fancy has created are those who assume a woman's shape with malicious intent, and then tempting men to marry them, devour them in the end, and all the children in the meantime produced." Other accounts of were-tigers (first cousins of werewolves) are found in the folklore of Southeast Asia, India, and elsewhere. This story also has echoes in such European tales as "The Swan Bride" or stories of the *selkies,* the magical creatures that appear as seals but can put off their skins and become beautiful women or handsome men. Some wed mortals, who find and conceal their magical skins. But most stories end with the *selkies* finding their hides, reclaiming their seal shapes, and either abandoning their human families or taking their children with them to live in the sea.

PEACOCK'S GHOST. Adapted from the narrative "Louisiana Ghost Story," in *Supernatural Tales from Around the World* (op. cit.). The original was printed in Fanny D. Bergen's article "Notes and Queries: Louisiana Ghost Story," *Journal of American Folk-Lore* 12 (1899). I have kept the thrust and language of the original tale, which is essentially the old woman's story. But I created the contemporary framing story, and held back the fact that the ghost is *female,* for an extra impact at the end.

ISRAEL AND THE WEREWOLF. Retold from a number of sources: *Tales of Terror: The Enchanted World,* by the Editors of Time-Life Books (Alexandria, Virginia: Time-Life Books, Inc., 1987), *Lilith's Cave: Jewish Tales of the Supernatural* by Howard Schwartz (New York: Oxford University Press, 1988), and *Classic Hasidic Tales* by Meyer Levin (New York: Citadel Press, 1966). Israel Ben Eliezer is the young man who became known as the Baal Shem Tov (Master of the Good Name). A renowned folk healer, mystic, and charismatic leader of the early Hasidic movement, he lived from 1700–1760. Many legends have grown up around this major Jewish teacher.

HOICHI THE EARLESS. Adapted and shortened from "The Story of Mimi-Nashi-Hoichi" by Lafcadio Hearn, in *Kwaidan: Stories and Studies of Strange Things* (Boston: Houghton Mifflin

Co., 1904; reprint, Rutland, Vermont: Charles E. Tuttle Company, Inc., 1971). Another reprint edition is available from Dover Books, New York. Hearn notes, "The *biwa*, a kind of four-stringed lute, is chiefly used in musical recitative. . . . The *biwa* is played with a kind of plectrum, called *bachi*, usually made of horn. . . . At Dan-no-ura, in the Straits of Shimonoseki, was fought the last battle of the long contest between the Heike, or Taira clan, and the Genji, or Minamoto clan. There the Heike perished utterly, with their women and children, and their infant emperor likewise. . . . And the sea and shore have been haunted for seven hundred years. . . . On dark nights thousands of ghostly fires hover above the beach, or flit above the waves—pale lights which the fisherman call *oni-bi*, or demon-fires."

A SNAP OF THE FINGERS. This is based on the story "The Calle Del Puente Del Cuervo" ("The Street of the Bridge of the Raven"), in *Legends of the City of Mexico*, by Thomas A. Janvier (New York: Harper & Brothers, 1910). "The raven was the guardian of the dead in Christian folklore. The body of St. Vincent was guarded from intruders by a raven. This connection with the dead made the raven a natural symbol of the devil, and St. Benedict reported that the devil appeared to him in the form of a raven. A legend narrated in the Koran (Surah V) says a raven was scratching 'the ground to show Cain how to hide his brother's body.' "—Anthony S. Mercatante, *Zoo of the Gods: Animals in Myth, Legend, & Fable* (op. cit.).

NARROW ESCAPE. I first heard this "urban legend" when I was a tenderfoot scout at a campout in the Redwood Regional Park in northern California. Since then, I have come across countless versions of the story. It is always presented as truth, as something that happened to "a friend of a friend of mine." Folklorist Jan Harold Brunvand gives a version from Utah in his book

The Vanishing Hitchhiker: American Urban Legends & Their Meanings (New York: W. W. Norton & Company, 1981). Two versions from Indiana, "Assailant in the Backseat Foiled by Truck Driver" and "Assailant in the Backseat Foiled by Station Attendant," are found in *Hoosier Folk Legends,* by Ronald L. Baker (Bloomington: Indiana University Press, 1982). I also found particularly helpful an Australian version of this widely traveled story, "The Killer in the Back Seat," in *The Book of Nasty Legends,* by David Austin (Boston: Routledge & Kegan Paul, 1983). It remains a favorite scary tale for campfire and sleepover telling.

THE BLACK FOX. This is a retelling of a legend presented in verse, "The Black Fox of Salmon River," by J. G. Brainard, reprinted in *A Book of New England Legends and Folk Lore In Prose and Poetry,* by Samuel Adams Drake (Boston: Little, Brown & Co., 1884, revised 1906; reprint, Rutland, Vermont: Charles E. Tuttle Company, Inc., 1971). Another, more elaborate version of the legend, also in verse, can be found in John Greenleaf Whittier's *Legends of New England* (1831; reprint, Baltimore: Clearfield Company, 1992). Whittier prefaces his own poem "The Black Fox" with the comment, "There is a strange legend relative to the 'Black Fox of Salmon River,' Connecticut . . . Brainard alludes to it in one of his finest poems: 'And there the Black Fox roved and howled and shook / His thick tail to the hunters.' "

THE MOTHER AND DEATH. I have adapted and considerably shortened the story originally published as "The Mother and the Dead Child." It is one of Hans Christian Andersen's more disturbing stories, sprinkled with startling images and a sense of the overwhelming power of destiny in human lives. The original can be found in any collection of his works that includes the author's more religious and allegorical pieces. A version of the complete text can also be found in *The Eerie Book* (op. cit.). For a somewhat similarly themed tale—the inevitability of one's fate—the reader might want to look at the Persian tale "Appointment in Samarra," which I have retold in *Even More Short & Shivery* (op. cit.).

About the Author

Robert D. San Souci is the award-winning author of many books for young readers, including *Short & Shivery, More Short & Shivery,* and *Even More Short & Shivery. School Library Journal* has called these books "an absolute delight. . . . Young readers will gobble up these thirty thrilling snacks and beg for more." Widely traveled and a popular speaker, Robert San Souci has lectured at schools, libraries, universities, and conferences in more than thirty states. A native Californian, he lives in the San Francisco Bay Area.